AF140681

FSC
www.fsc.org

MIX

Papier aus ver-
antwortungsvollen
Quellen
Paper from
responsible sources

FSC® C105338

Dieter Gerhard

Follow the sun

Love till all eternity

**An extraordinary story
about love and affection,
about reason and emotion,
about tragedy and grief,
on the end and the beginning**

Photo envelope side: Gerhard Vohs "wedding
rings"

Bibliographic information of the German national library:

The German national library registers this publication in the German national bibliography; specified bibliographic data are retrievable on the Internet about http://dnb.dnb.de.

© 2014 name of the author / legal owner:

Dieter Gerhard

Illustration: Dieter Gerhard

Production and publishing company: BoD – Books on Demand, Norderstedt, Germany

ISBN: 978-3-7357-2175-4

Table of contents:

Follow the sun
Love till all eternity

1. Thoughts that tormented me

There are the thoughts that plagued me helpless to sit and reach for you, to take you in his arms; to show you that you're not alone. But all I can do is thinking of you and hope that you understand my thoughts.

Tears formed in my eyes and made me helpless because I do not know if I had told you often enough how much I love you, adore you; you're my everything; I can feel the feeling of emptiness in me, if you're not with me.

I am delivered to the loneliness, feels me helplessly paralyzed, how a victim. At the supermarket only ready-to-serve meals are bought if generally and are used in the kitchen only a knife, a little board and a cup. It is the cup which you had given me at last, a cup with a heart formed from fingers and the individual message "365 days of love for yourself". It is rinsed, like the other things, immediately after use again, so that I can use them the next day again.

The refrigerator, once filled with lots of goodies, today only knows margarine, packaged bread and one or two bottles of beer.

Washed laundry is drawn as again as it comes from the washing machine or from the dryer. Only no circumstances make.

Books I have even bought myself to read them and to deflect myself with the contents a little. They are patient and put no questions.

I read even the advertisement which overcrowded weekly the mailbox recently carefully. Sometimes I speak even, besides, indiscernibly, softly and quietly. The flowers at least seemed to like my soliloquies; they caught all at once in excessively to blossom.

After work, I always go straight home; it is enough if I was working in the job. At home, I live in my own world; love to run around in casual clothes and myself on Sunday not to attract more properly, preferring to walk through the apartment in pajamas, unshaven, unkempt. These can drink as coffee, all day watching TV and eating, in between a couple of biscuits, instead sumptuous lunch.

My life that I lead now is quiet, calm and protected, protected from questions with pity and terrible feelings before.

It is the loneliness, a forest fire one with a counter fire fought which makes out-of-touch, strangely and shy and in the exchange with the world one has gone down on a minimum. The phone is quiet, in the mailbox only daily papers and advertisement and e-mails check that it is enough if one once a month makes. These are thus and thus only Spams they appear, publicity campaigns in masses were dispatched. They land everybody unread in the wastepaper basket.

I myself need no more people, no friends and no relatives. If I go alone through the town and come again home, I know that one can live quite well on an obliterated earth without perishing in the loneliness.

Will therefore continue to live with my self-talk, the words that are very familiar to me and do not speak again; will continue to throw my gaze back and pull résumé of the past, think about which projects and goals we had set ourselves.

But if you have lived together for years with someone and now lives alone, then it's actually quite a painful condition. You can hear the silence in a candlelit room, the unpredictable ticking of a clock; the noise of the wind on the balcony; sees the restless moving of shadows on the opposite wall; feel the empty apartment, which was previously filled with harmony, love and happiness.

Now, unfortunately, everything has changed. The nice dream is finished; the luck has left me, an endless time without you have begun. The nice hours, the recollections, every still so small moment, everything forget, everything worthless, all shit. It would be better to live together with his mortal enemy, than to give up itself to the horror of the loneliness. However, I have decided so and must go this way.

It's boring without you, a yawning boredom, feel dissatisfied. It is an inner discontent that makes me listless and where I know what to do with me.

No ideas in the head which irritate to one to move them and also no aim in the eye that one possibly wants to reach.

Maybe it is just one message wants to inspire me to find an answer to my questions; on my questions what I want what I should start with my time; what is important to me. However, what has the future for a value if you are not present.

The television is also not as entertaining any more as earlier. Only people the anecdotes from her especially thrilling life tell and pull this particularly grievously in the length.

Cannot remind me at all of it, when I had seen sometimes a good film last, not there are no good films, however, everything shimmers what about the screen, are repetitions of second-class and third-rate films and people-going goofy entertainment shows. Maybe I see even in such a way, I do not know it.

In the evening I lie in the bed, look to your side and feels for you. Your place is cold and empty, no breath I feels, only one picture of you sees and goes to ruin in sadness.

I think of you and ask myself how it just probably goes out to you whether I see once again a sign of you. I know that my thoughts land from time to time with you, you have often enough confirmed it to me.

Only recently you had visited me again when I was to the work. I came home and it burnt light in the bedroom. First it had surprised me a little, particularly as it was a light bright day. However, then I knew that it could be only you. It was the bedside table lamp on your side which was switched on. Also the next day you visited me and turned on the light, as well as on the next days. Sometimes you came if I was at home in the sitting room and I could not note it. Only when I went to the bedroom, I saw the light again in was.

I had been glad, about your visit because I knew that you wanted to show with the fact that you would also miss me.

You had already visited me some months ago; there you had turned on one of three stool lights in the sitting room, always the same, on the right behind in the corner. It is ordinarily switched like the others by remote control about radio outlets.

At night now and again you also came, had switched on the lamp in the sitting room again from whose light I woke up then. Then on the couch we sat and talked, rather we exchanged our thoughts.

At that time, as the first time the lamp shone as me home came, I thought in burglars, black dressed with black color in the face. Immediately I reached for an object, a screen and crept in the direction of sitting room. Round me was a silence, an awfully silence. It was not the silence which originates if everybody slept in a house, no; it was another silence, a menacing silence.

My heart was pounding wildly and irregularly. I sneaked in sweat ahead, not daring to breathe, trying to organize my thoughts. Thirst overcame me, my mouth was parched, an uncomfortable feeling with a sickening taste on the tongue. What if the intruder is armed, if there is a murderer or even a kidnapper, I thought.

With the umbrella I could not frighten him probably sometimes; still I took together my whole courage to position myself to the intruder, to expel maybe him what seemed to me with exact consideration rather dubious.

I briefly considered whether I should put back the umbrella again and take a more actual weapon, a knife, a big butcher's knife, instead, maybe.

No! Now I had come so far if now I turn back, I would not have ventured it once more; probably I would have cleared out before fear.

Slowly I crept on, peeked around the corner through the open door, but could see nothing, only the stool light that radiated brightness in the corner. I clutched the umbrella more firmly with the hand and rushed me into the room. But there was no one, no ransacked drawers and cabinets open, no slit sofa cushions and torn cable, as it is known from gangster films ago.

The next day the light was again in and thus my supposition on the neighbor went to ruin under me who tries out his science with pleasure in radio controls. Possibly his radio frequency disturbs my remote control, releases a signal over and over again what is taken up by the radio outlets. However, a further inquiry with my neighbor proved the opposite.

Only at a substantially later time came to me the enlightenment that it could have been only you. Yes, you visited me at the most different times and I know, how much you me miss acts, just as I do it. Only we could not see ourselves, do not embrace, perceive only the feeling that we are together.

Your sporadic visits gave me the feeling of nearness all the same in which situation I just was be for ever and ever connected with the heart with his favorite ones, no matter where you were also.

My days pointlessly moved along as if you had never been as if was what we have experienced only one illusion, only one imagination, a longing. I am alone you are not any more with me, however, the recollections which I carry like a precious present in myself wake up over and over again; recollections they point, how much I miss you, how much I admired you, how much I still love you.

If I had a wish freely, I would wish no fame or wealth, no expensive cars, no big villa, no thick bank account. I would only wish that everything would be in such a way as it was former.

It's hard not to see you, to enjoy all the beautiful moments with such wonderful people. It will never be the same again; they are memories, memories of perfect times that I spent with you. Do you remember our picnic in the car park?

2. An exceptional Dinner

It was Monday, in the morning one day where I am on the move, actually, quite early to visit my operational area. As a field representative of a large-scale enterprise I am on the move mostly the whole week and spend the night regularly in the space Hannover.

However, today I had one more discussion in my local office. The discussion was quicker than planned past and because one would expect me only in the late afternoon, I had the need to see you before once more and to surprise you with something, maybe with special food.

My image needs a certain preparation and because I live in a detached house arrangement where houses were so built that the complex resembled an atrium, the contact with the other neighbors was also connected with tender friendship where taking and giving was connected with a lot of self-evident fact.

Thus I called the woman of my neighbor and asked them to lend her bistro set to me.

»Why you still are at home, I thought today you wanted to go to Hannover,« she asked.

»Yes this already, it moves around a few hours and I wanted to use the remaining time for a surprise for what I could use your garden pieces of furniture again.«

»What you want then with it, nevertheless, you have yourself which!«

»Yes this already, but I needs a little more elegant pieces of furniture which I can transport by the car and there I thought of the small folding table with the folding chairs which stand with you in the pond. I need them only today, for one to two hours, then bring back I them to you again. If you lent then still your picnic basket to me, I would be connected to you very much.«

»This is no problem, you can fetch them any time, do not need to bring back them also immediately again, this has time. What surprise is it then? Certainly infected because a woman behind.«

»Is not so curious! You will find out it absolutely early enough. On the other hand it is also better if you do not find out it, if my surprise goes to the trousers. Nevertheless, you know who has the damage, does not need to provide for the mockery.«

Thus I drove off, fetched on the way the pieces of furniture, called occasionally still with the Chinese and found me shortly after on the company area of your employer. The parking bay was not filled excessively and thus I chose one which offered me the direct look to the entrance.

I got out of the boot of my car then the small round folding table and two matching chairs. The table got an almost full-length white table cover on which I placed plate and cutleries exactly oppositely, as well as two wineglasses for the white dry Chateau Grand Vin, with representative, qualitatively reliable Cuvee from the province Bordeaux. The warmest recommendation of the shop assistant of our village wine action for my forthcoming happening.

Candles flickered on the table, quiet music resounded from the loudspeakers of the car radio and a red rose draped your plate. A look at the clock betrayed to me, at ten minutes your lunch break begins to check through everything over again.

Table cover was OK, plates were confronted, spoons and forks besides, wineglasses were right at the spoon point, candles burnt in the light wind and the radio played subdued music.

The wine stands handy and …,

Shit there she was embarrassing again, my thoughtlessness, my inattentiveness, my absent-mindedness, how. I had forgotten the corkscrew, see him still before me lying on the sitting room table and now could miss to me a finish.

I wondered what I could do now. Maybe run the company, ask them in the canteen and after a device for uncorking the wine bottle, then one way. But where is the canteen, how do I get me without the security service also transported there involuntarily again.

Maybe I should apply the Indian's method, the cork squash into, however, then he would push over and over again before the bottle opening and an eternity would last, until the first glass is filled.

Then a video occurred to me whom I had seen on the Internet, while a man him had the same problem like I and a bottle opened without corkscrew. He upholstered the bottle ground and hit in several times against a tree. The cork was done by the pushes slowly from the bottle.

Thus I took the bottle, the tin foil capsule removed, upholstered the bottle with a few paper-napkins and hit evenly by light trains on the parking bay paving.

First happened nothing at all and I had fear that the bottle will immediately shatter to me, however, then seem to function. The cork moved really step by step from the bottleneck, until I seized him with the fingers and could seesaw the rest with light torn in halves and here movements out.

Joyfully I swayed in the hips that everything ran so perfectly, only the Chinese was still absent whom I had ordered for shortly after twelve. Again I looked at the clock, three minutes before twelve to visit you time. When I was on the hall to your job, I saw you standing there. Behind you a man who was about to massage your cervical muscles.

I shut to you both and shouted with restrained voice:

»Hey!«

Startled you turned round, saw me and ran to me in the arms. Besides, you asked:

»Hey Darling, I thought you would be for a long time on the highway.«

Your eyes had far burst, bent the eyebrows inwards and your face emitted cheerfulness, relaxation and joy of life.

»Oh I thought, make a small detour to see what you do thus the whole day. Finally, me am away a whole week and do not know sometimes like you your spare time without myself spends.«

»However, this is dear from you that you visit me here,« you replied.

I took you a little aside to escape from the listening in ears of your colleague and asked:

»The guy who had bothered just your shoulders, who this that?«

»Oh,« I heard you saying and you pulled an eyebrow far upwards. »Do I note there may be a light jealousy?«

»What I jealously, how you get on then. I am only a little curious, further nothing. Jealously …, I … ha-ha … YES! Who was the guy.«

»Darling, you need to you do not worry, this is only one colleague him is spoken for and feels from own gender drawn,« you whispered to me in the ear.

»OK, well! Subject does. I have there sometimes a question to you. How do stand the chances to kidnap you to a small snack?«

»You at the moment we hang up to the neck in work and …«

»This makes nothing,« I interrupted and took you in the arm with outward. On the parking bay just a scooter whose box on the carrier carried the promotional label of a

Chinese from the closer surroundings drove up, carefully followed your eyes the driver who stopped directly before the covered table and looked around expectantly.

»I believe, I have to go there sometimes over here.« if I mentioned, let go you and went towards in the run to the supplier.

He gave me the calculation which I studied shortly after; my purse pulled out and got out money.

»Many thanks the rest are for them,« spoke to him, took food what embedded it was in a plastic bag and waved you to me.

The scooter started, started moving and now only you recognized the run of the things. With far being open eyes and a slightly open mouth you got closer, examined the table and asked:

»What is all that?«

I opened the cover of the aluminum menu bowls and presented:

»Crispy duck Szechuan style with brown sauce and some vegetables.«

»I do not know what I should say,« you spoke very much in amazement.

»You could say: thanks, you are a God among the men, a hero among the warriors, and a prince among the thieves.«

»This looks here thus like a scene in an old film. Vantage point …, second …, this is a scene from an old film …, or?«

»Completely it comes on it. Do you know the old films with Gerry Grant, from the forties and fifties years?«

»So old films I do not know.«

»OK, then here this is a perfect independent, self-thought up, masterly idea on which I have come without foreign help.«

Smiling you looked again at the table, looked every detail most exactly, emitted an enthusiasm and meant:

»What are your doing with me? If you do not believe that there also shops are the dishes and drinks offer without being put out to the exhaust gases by cars and without looks full of envy of my colleagues. You are crazy.«

»Does move? Yes to me, moves after you.«

You came round the table, sat down on my lap and have kissed me. It was one of these kisses again which provided for tingling creeps, for startled insects to my belly and all of a sudden I was delivered to the interplay of the feelings unrestrained.

»Come lets us eat,« I spoke to you, »otherwise, your lunch break is over and you have still taken no mouthful to yourself.«

I let my gaze wander along the building front, a front that consisted mainly of glass. Actually to some windows were women and men who were watching us and what is happening down here. A few waved, thinking of an advertising campaign, a hoax, or even a television debut; others are likely to provide only an idiot who makes a fool of oneself.

We sat, ate, talked a after another, as if we had not seen each other for years. All around us seemed to forget everything the company parking lot, office building, people who saw us here, sometimes shaking his head walked past.

It was like a romantic Candle Light dinner under a private pavilion, directly on one beach with fine-sandy sand. Round us everything was wonderful, with a lot of charm and a very reassuring atmosphere. These are moments which one keeps longer in the heart and also in memory which one remembers over and over again with pleasure, sometimes expects even longingly these wonderful hours in twos.

However, also this moment approaches the end to. We had already covered the lunch break and also for me it became a time to go my way. Hannover shouted and the way was wide. Before, I had to return the garden furniture and even the picnic basket.

»Not be sad,« I spoke to you. »If I am at the hotel, I call you and at the latest on Friday I am there again.«

»Till Friday is still long what I should do in the interim without you.«

»Darling, even if our ways separate, we know with certainty that they will also find themselves. With two souls are so close as ours, the distance and the time of the separation plays a secondary role.«

Again it was your kiss which tore me totally from the road which was so warm that with me the luck hormones played up. So a kiss can say absolutely more than thousand words could describe it generally.

Yes I love you, can catch it hardly in words. It is your smile that over and over again the sun did magic in my heart; your look which showed me that you love me; the gestures which expressed welcome and closeness; the hand on my shoulder which showed with that I am alone not; the spoken words, affectionately and, nevertheless, of full honesty; to be quiet sometimes also, unites with the knowledge which words are superfluous at some moments; the embrace which states that we always are there for each other.

»I call you if I have come. Then at the latest on Friday we see again and think of it, one must always keep to himself a little luck, until one can shut again in the arms.«

»I love you,« you still had to me in the ear whispering and then have gone. I still looked at you, until you disappeared in the building, then I removed everything together, brought back the garden pieces of furniture and transferred me on the highway.

After two hours of driving, I reached Hanover, kept me briefly in the office and then drove on to my lodging facility. It was an out of town hotel, with hospitable atmosphere polite, middle-class food and nature-loving environment.

»To see again, hello, nicely them,« the doorkeeper welcomed me. »I hope them had a pleasant journey.«

»Thanks of the inquiry, was not much off on the highway. What have they to offer today in dinner?«

»Beforehand a clear oxtail soup, as a main way a Lower Saxony plate with light wild minced meat steak, potato croquettes, champignons and red cabbage. As a dessert: Cinnamon star ice.«

»Oh, this well sounds. I make me only a little fresh and then come down me. They can already tap to me a beer.«

After I had signed the registration, I proceeded on the room. It was same, as usual; the same bed, the same curtains and the same look in the front garden. I sat down on the bed and called you:

»Hey treasure, I am it …, I have arrived safely …, am already on my room …, today no I have no appointments, only tomorrow again and this richly. Will eat yet a little thing, drink one, two little beers and look through a few documents which I need for my acquisition. … Make I treasure …, I also love you! Sleep well.«

The next morning I went as first in the local office, because after the job as a managerial authorized representative I was still a department manager of a small group of specialists. Their job is under others to be not only a contact of the customers lying in the vicinity, but also to organize appointments on site for me to acquire new business and also new connections.

To increase the new business continuously is the significant job of a field representative. In addition the managers lie to me in the nape who lure with extremely attractive shares in profits. Up to now I had achieved my aims without problems; however, this luck will not always be on my side.

A jump would be possibly now the right moment, now where I have got to know you. On a continuing basis it would be no good company if I am on the move the whole week.

3. You were something special

The meeting with you was the nicest what could happen to me. In the midst of a tumultuous period of life you have smiled at me and have crept into my heart, stuck on me with your warmth.

In the warmth of your eyes, your affection had been reflected. Banter has brought me to the laughter and the first talks pointed me which trust you gave me.

Your presence illuminated my day and it was pleasant over and over again if we acted playfully in such a way, as if we quarreled and allowed never to fall into oblivion, besides, the laughter.

Completely at the beginning you had put to me a question which occupied me at that time very much.

It was on a Friday, a day where my travel activity had for this week ended. Already about midday I went back, had an almost empty highway before myself and was happy to see you soon. Tender publishing companies on something being and, nevertheless, absentee; a longing to one consumes; a desire for the big feeling you gave me.

My whole body caught again in to tingle and warmed up my heart when I stood before your door and rang halting. It lasted longer than, otherwise, possibly you do not expect me yet. I rang the second spot, laid my ear at the side to the door to be able to perceive noises in the internal one of the flat better. However, it was quiet.

It seemed in such a way, as if you were not, but, nevertheless, I had just still seen your car before the door, or? Do you possibly sleep and on the light bright day?

Suddenly I heard behind myself a voice, a voice to me was familiar and for which I longed. It was your voice which asked at the same time joyfully and surprised:

»Darling, you are there already?«

»Yes, I have cheated with my working hours a little because I wanted you sometimes earlier than, otherwise, with the presence of my presence to dull ones.«

Affectionately you laid your arms around my neck and softly our lips touched. Your fingertips disappeared in my hairline and carefully your fingernails scratch in my nape.

It was simply divine to have so near you, to feel your lips, to feel your hair and your kiss to taste which kindled a passion which brought the fuel in me for blazing.

Then you opened the front door and spoke at the same time:

»You could never bore me.«

Besides, quite warmly became to me around the heart and I hoped that it becomes always so his that we would never lie side by side like railroad tracks.

We sat on the couch, heard music and I told about my job, about the field service, from other towns and about the wintry dangers which lurked outdoors on the highways. Quite firmly I held you in the arms and we laughed at our ideas which got involved in mad spinning mills. It is an irony that we both used with the knowledge that each of us understood it and even was able to answer. These were partly profound and playfully talks, also, however, also pensive and stupid ones.

However, then you interrupted my flow of words, laid your hand on my mouth and spoke:

»What we do here actually, Darling.«

I was a little confused about this statement, this statement about this confession that I could think of nothing else than to ask:

»Dull I you with my gossip?«

»No this not, but we are more than one month together and do you not find also peculiar that we have not gone on up to now yet?«

You spoke briskly and brought me further and further into embarrassment.

»You mean away from the field service, purely in the inside service, in a leading position or thus?«

»No, I mean sex, you silly. Did you may be interested in?«

I had been surprised at this openness a little, did not know like I should react to meet a direct question with a direct answer. To win a little time and to think I said a little bit halting:

»Oh …, sex …, clearly …!«

»Yes exactly. I also have the feeling and, nevertheless, we have not done it yet. You do not work like somebody who waits needlessly long.«

I was in a first-like conflict, was immediately surrounded by three catchwords, from feeling, from activities and unnecessary waiting. I had to think, let me think of something without offending you. Certainly, my wish close to take the certain step even dreamed at night of how I do it, but I held back again and again.

»Maybe it comes along that you remind me of my sister,« I lied to you before.

»You hurry said, you would be an only child.«

»Oh yes, is right!«

»I get maybe a serious answer, …please!«

You spoke easily irritated, still with an entertaining smile on the lips, but a little sensitively.

I believed myself, as if I had got lost as a secondary school pupil in a high school and stood now before the rector to fetch my punishment because I had forgotten to make my homework.

Thus I spoke honestly and from the deepest hearts:

»Is not angry at me, but I want to rush nothing.«

»You would have done this if it had been after the first date. The eleventh date and nothing happens, offends against the general action rules.«

»Who is doing only what he has always done, gets only what he has always got, "I said to you. "... And although it had its good points, so I want it now rather have to start all different.«

»OK, but you should know if you are so far, I am it also.«

Nevertheless, there was to think very much to me what you said me. Absolutely, there were already many mares who wanted to lure the stallion of the pasture, but which were not blest one with the God-given appearance, with the other one would rather enter into the celibacy, have called some than the best friend the anorexia in her life, then still the women are there a lot talk and, besides, say nothing and the rest wants after a shit experience which one pulls out them of the marsh.

However, with you it was different; you were a woman where one must owe God that one had come into the world as a man.

I went the next day to my best friend to Marc. I needed someone who could give me some advice; someone listened to me, understood me and even longer knew, without coming to any ulterior motives. Maybe it was just the proximity I was looking for, easy to talk with a friend to talk trash from the soul.

»Hey, you I have not seen long. You do not visit me certainly from nothing but politeness,« I heard saying from Marc when he opened the door to me.

»No, I need sometimes your advice.«

»Oh just from me« he said. »Come first purely.«

»Likes a beer,« he asked me on the way in the sitting room.

»No to thanks, for myself,« I did not answer and took burst.

»What advice needs then just from me.«

»Well, the alternative would have been your brother, but because he handles with women not quite well, I thought. At the moment I am in a quite peculiar situation. It is about a special woman …,«

»In a peculiar situation,« Marc interrupted me questioningly and I noted an urgent curiosity in his eyes. Many years we knew ourselves and always one was he whose advice did not circumscribe exactly really, but any more, more outlines, were illustrated not to commit itself.

»Yes peculiarly. It is in such a way, we already meet since some time and up to now we have not done this yet what I would have already done, usually actually, much earlier.«

It stamped in a break, an interruption of our exchange of ideas with a silence that one could hear, actually, the thoughts of the other with exact listening. Then I got a picture from my purse and showed it to Marc.

»She is really a sharp woman. Up to now

you believed, nevertheless, that a long-term relationship limits itself to a week-end and now something so?«

»I have resolved to lead in future a lasting monogamous respect«

»Where did you meet them?«

»I had seen them on a party and simply did not leave the eyes any more of her.«

»And this impressed they?« asked Marc.

»Apparently! Impressively I thought that we could talk and everybody something accept had. Most women talk about things and fallen out existences, but to the evening I had felt patriotic and thus we arranged to meet.«

»I may ask then sometimes, why this has not taken place yet what took place, otherwise, much earlier.«

»Yes, um … because to me this special woman is so extremely important I held for better to let concern the thing quietly and this is absolutely a new territory for me. But from a certain time, one should increase the tempo, or?«

»Now, she is for engaging?«

I nodded, thought at this moment again of you how unique you were for me as the bridge of our trust hardened more and more; how you got to touch me with easy simple words; to show me with animal looks how you love me.

»Is it your opinion, charming, adorable, lovable and friendly?«

Again I nodded.

»Does she correspond to your taste, does it have brains, and is it able?«

Nodding I affirmed everything, besides, though still of you, of your interesting eyes, your nice lips and above all of your radiation, harmony, charm, strength, to your sure appearance and the important conversations which we carried on.

»So, what's the problem,« interrupted me Marc in my thoughts.

I considered, thought about the words of Marc, a little said, however, a lot brought. However, long waiting makes only impatience with itself stand the inability in a queue, endure, be patient and thus I had made my decision. Still head nodding I got up and went, while Marc to me still shouted behind:

»Good luck and ... would be nice if you notify us of times imagine. Would love to see who has managed to cut down the gnarled oak, which now drives down the river to the other timber. That I can still see that the loggers shouting respect, I never thought.«

It was already late; still I decided to drive myself to you. I stood before your front door, confirmed the bell and waited. After fairly long time you opened the door and something spoke surprised:

»Hey Darling.«

»I hope, you have not slept yet.«

»I also have not. Come on in.«

You wore a white bathrobe, a toweling-like garment without fastener which was held together with a bandage belt. In the sitting room on the couch you cuddled up so close to me that without fail my looks landed in your cutting. I was not able differently and it was nice what I saw there, I liked it. You asked:

»Where were you today?«

»I was with a friend, had to talk with him about what.«

»And how was your conversation,« what I answered to:

»…, humph, you know the chain saw massacre?«

»The original or the Remix?«

»Both.« if I mentioned enthusiastically, although I must admit that I knew neither one nor other.

»Neither,« you declined.

I took a deep breath and expelled them in the same breath by the nose again and my chest rebelled totally and collapsed afterwards again in itself.

»It was so similar, only suitable and how was it with you?«

»This day was such a middle thing between boredom and vacation make, linked with distinctive sluggishness, listlessness and tiredness what I had also used completely.«

Besides, you had this again smile and your eyes glittered in the light of the candles which you had kindled in numerous amount on the table.

»You are not only lovely, but also are still clever,« I mentioned.

»And why you do not kiss me then,« you ordered to me.

»Oh man, you can read in addition still thought.«

I could renounce everything, on breakfast, lunch and supper; on work, money earn and luxury, on my car, my house, my bank, however, not on one of your kisses. You had such a sex appeal, were so unlikely and with your movement, your elegance, the litheness you challenged me to never be able to resist yourself. It was like a high rope act with which one had the feeling to float between sky and earth. You had enjoyed this play with the seduction and it was amusing for me as you irritated me.

What had taken place earlier much earlier, now took place and every touch of you was like an arcing, every movement like an exploding fire pot and every excitement like a highly spraying volcano eruption.

A play of the passion and desire began, until it broke upon us. Tensely, trembling, vibrating; a quake ran through to my body and like a panting dog I snapped at air.

Exhausted I dropped my head in the cushion and minutes of the silence entered, combined with the knowledge that words were just superfluous. I thought of myself, of our respect which showed in the most miraculous way that we had found together a little bit very much valuable. It was wonderful to feel you so near and to know that just it had become a part of my life.

4. Fears of getting too involved?

When I woke in the morning, you lay there like the goddess Venus, how a recumbent act in a piece of art of Pierre Auguste Renoir. Your arm covered the breast and did with it a sexily play with the concealed. I admired your hourglass figure, this velvet-soft skin, the miraculous curvatures and I inhaled the odoriferous smell of your body deeply. You were nice, thrilling, desirable, amusing and perfectly shaped and in me the glow caught again in to blaze, like the burning of a chimney which slowly rises to a fire.

We lay even longer time in the bed and I told anecdotes from my life how I had taken part for years as a courageous cowboy in authentic things in west club, enjoyed in the evening with guitar the campfire mood and dropped myself every now and then with the Bull Riding of gone through horses down.

»And I should believe this you everything what you tell me there everything,« you had expressed yourself disbelieving.

»This is true everything,« I protested.

»You play the guitar?«

»Eric Clapton, Chuck Berry and Jimi Hendrix are nothing against it.«

»You have a colt?«

»The replica of a percussion revolver, caliber 44, 1848 Mod with blue sapphire imitation in the grips.«

»And have also ridden you?«

»Well, one needs no special qualification in addition. It is enough if one has a distinctive voice, so that one can shout according to Yahoo or Yippy-Ay-Yaeh.«

»To ride on a bull?«

» Um ..., more or less on a mechanical bull. But they are wilder than real cops, have still the scars from my last ride.«

»Where?« you asked, as if you did not believe me and I had to present a suitable proof. I felt under the cover for your hand, took them and led them to a scar close in my hip. However, she came from a barbed wire injury which I had got as a teenager when I had liked backward against one of these wire points in a fence.

»There they are, my heavy traumatic injuries,«

I sank your fingertips about the stigma and I felt a sensational pleasant and velvety prank feeling.

»Oh,« you spoke had surprised and after you had stroked them extensively, you asked: »Should I kiss them, so that she leaves?«

I believe, you could really read thought, because I wished nothing more at this moment, than to feel your lips on my body. Thus I answered:

» Just do what you think is right. I'll hardly stop them.«

Softly your lips touched the scar. It was like silk on the skin and I went into a ride to happiness. To have it was so beautiful that it seemed to me almost in disbelief, so done a stroke of luck to you.

When you appeared under the cover again, our lips melted themselves with each other and empathy, excitement and sentimentality joined. I could introduce with no nice place on earth to listen in as your respiration here.

When our lips separated, you looked to me in the eyes, a firm deep look which bored up to my heart by.

»You probably like this,« I mentioned what you answered flattering:

»This is like an addiction.«

I spent the morning with you, enjoyed it like you spoilt me and I let it go out about myself. Tomorrow, however, about midday I had to pack fast to myself home, already my pocket for the trip.

»In am there in at the latest two hours again and then we go to the Greek.«

The stacks of my pocket ran as a matter of routine rather fast and also the compilation of various documents went for me quickly from the hand.

When I came back I was overwhelmed and I noticed nothing else as a:

»Wow,« to say.

You had buckled in bowl and looked simply charming. The knee-length black dress, optimally stressed your figure. Your neck decorated a discreet, but pretty chain and your low neckline granted to me insights which inspired my imagination immediately.

»At what do you look me so funnily, do I have …, spinach between the teeth or what?«

Besides, you looked at me and I stood there before nothing but amazement, like a puppet figure, with open mouths and folded down jaw.

»Um …, I will rather say probably …, or what,« I answered.

»You look as if you did not have all the dishes in the cupboard.«

»Not all dishes in the cupboard? Yaeh.«

I still looked at you, was enthusiastically from your appearance, from your clothing, from your sex appeal that you emitted.

»If to you does not occur any more, you are able quietly your mouth again to make,« you replied to me and gave me a slap under the chin.

»Wow,« I said to myself and crept behind you to the car.

We drove off and because there was as expected no parking bay before the restaurant, I went in in the multi-store car park. I studied under the abandonment of the building already the prize board and sneered for the moment at the high fees.

»Two euros the hour, this is usury. Does the owner have an army of illegitimate children, or why does so much money need?«

»Do not get excited about the paltry amount on. Who can eat out, who can afford a couple of parking fees,« are you trying to encourage me even though the price was really a pure daylight robbery.

The Greeks were not overly stuffed. A good place in a secluded corner was found. The candlelight on the table was your smiling blue eyes and long eyelashes that received by a mascara pen a wonderful swing, a very special form of expression.

I was about again to give noteworthy and typical occurrences from my lives to the best; if a history told about a friend who had, actually, everything: Own house, enough money, a pretty friend and in a diagnosis of an incurable genetic defect almost to reason would have gone.

These are my reinforced communication needs, the grief of a field representative who tries with this successful fight sport to express his verbal strengths, how the embodiment of a market crier in word skill and enthusiasm.

»After you have introduced me according to all rules of the art in the exercise of the activity of a travelling salesman; me has persuaded of the fact that the occupation is more than only one job, now the time has come that I put sometimes a few questions to you.«

» Well then shooting times going.«

»All right! How a quite sweet and anyway very winning type creates it like you, though a few quite bad parodies on it has …,

»I do not know what you mean,« I interrupted you.

»... how he manages to be as long as a single?«

»Oh you want to put a right question. Oh you fright …, this is really a right question. Um …, O-k-a-y …!« I considered a moment and then spoke further: »What do you hold from fears of getting too involved?«

»Fears of getting too involved? Humph …, do not buy me from you,« you replied and turned with the thumb and forefinger the handle of your wineglass to and fro.

»Really not and why not?« I wanted to know.

»The last hour at least one dozen pretty and extremely attractive women have gone past here certainly and you have appreciated them of no look.«

I turned, looked in all directions, looked for these extremely attractive women whom I had appreciated supposedly of no look, possibly because I had not noted them yet sometimes. As a result I meant:

»Oh no, but you obviously already or I have misunderstood there something.«

You caught in amusing to smile. Besides, your eyebrows and the nostrils next lifted themselves a little. The cheek bones came out more intensely pulled the corners of mouth upwards and left your eyelids deform to slit. There was no bigger power than the power of the laughter and particularly from you which was dangerously contagious.

You had the nicest laughter that I had ever seen, with this pleased glitter in the eyes which was there still if your laughter has become long ago one smiling.

»You should make only no hope to yourself,« you said, took your glass, drank a gulp and continued the sentence: »I am very much …, very conventional woman.«

»Clear! How is proper, finally, also for a woman.«

You had taken my hand, held on them with your both hands, stroked with the thumb my back of the hand and noted:

»You have not answered yet my question.«

»To your question?«

»Yes on my question!«

»OK …, OK …, you know …, I believe I wait simply patiently to the right woman comes.«

As a result you had looked around in the space, got stuck with every look at almost every occupied table, sounded out the guests and the staff and asked:

»And …, you think …, you will find them here?«

Smiling you moistened with the tongue yours delicate pink lips, glided softly with the fingertips over it, bit to you gently on the lower lip and sank, besides, your humid fingertips about the neck to the collarbone and again back. My eyes pursued the events and tiny elevations on the skin let me like a plucked chicken look. I took your other hand, kissed every single fingertip and spoke:

»I become more confident from day to day.«

5. Valentine's Day, Day of the lovers

On the weekends I enjoyed being together with you. For this Sunday you had ordered a table in your favorite Chinese. When we got there, our table was not free, so I went to the counter and got our appetizers ever. Everlasting you were on the phone, watch test over to me and there was a shiver-inspiring smile of yours. When I came up with the drinks on you, you finished your conversation simultaneously. We raised our glasses to what you said:

»It was my friend girl, she has stress with her man.«

»Why, I have asked? «I replied to you.

»No, not that. But the question stood in your eyes«

»Ah,« I mentioned, looked at you imploringly and admired the color of your sky-blue eyes in which the dim light of the Chinese silk lamps was reflected. Also your face shone in a special shine and even our drinks shone in an amber-colored tone.

»And what do they ask then now?« I protested.

You attached me, let your look in my eyes jump to and fro and spoke questioningly:

»Let's break down the food?«

»You are unbelievable,« I found out, »how do you make this only?«

»It is always this resembles with you. You want to eat this allow to always fall out, but not today, I am in starving.«

»I feel the same way.« And I tried to kiss you tenderly on the neck. But you evaluate from, saw me with an exciting eyelashes and my test:

»First we eat.«

In the meantime, our table became free, a place directly at the window with look at the illuminated discs of the surrounding flats and the asphalted street in which the road lighting was reflected. Now and then the vehicles went by the night dusk which revealed the drizzle of the rain in the floodlight.

I looked at you, admired you admired this rare gem that had been fighting in my heart.

»You look charming,« I said.

Appreciative and, nevertheless, something move you accepted the compliment, looked, besides, with slightly lowered head to your lap and meant:

»If you like my new dress, I have bought it only yesterday.«

»I do not speak of your dress,« I mentioned and to me to my disgrace I noted only then how fantastically this dress stood to you, nevertheless.

»I mine you, my treasure.«

I was to be had noted to the opinion a small discoloration in your face when these words stepped in the sphere of your consciousness. A helpless, undecided situation which inclines to it watches over and over again there and way and at the same time to my looks to make way, linked with an affectionate smile.

»Thanks,« you spoke completely move. Our food came and a variety of prepared dishes spoilt our palate. On this occasion, the cook can fall back on a true cornucopia of the spices which the goods basket of the Chinese agriculture puts at possession. It was a treat of every admirer of Asian cuisine.

On clearing the table you got a box from your handbag and laid them on the table.

»What this is,« I asked.

»You are on the move Wednesday somewhere again in Lower Saxony and Wednesday, nevertheless, is Valentine's Day.«

Rest entered for seconds and I noticed that something was out of place for me here.

»Oh …, Valentine's Day …, he always comes every year so fast …, do you also not find?«

A silly precarious situation, the day where you retaliate with romantic, original and unusual love confessions to show how happy you loved ones. Ironically, the day I have even forgotten.

»My present to you …, um …, still lies in the business,« then I further spoke, »… because I have not bought t …, um … yet, … Excuses.«

You smiled at me, as if you had known it already before and spoke with affectionate words:

»If you know, Darling, you do not believe at all as nicely it is to be with somebody together not to lie sometimes tried with such little things. So and now open up the box.«

»Oh, it is not only the box. I just wanted to say, thus I have never seen a nice box.«

I moved at an end of the loop on which freed itself of the knots, picked up the lid and had been surprised. An extremely elegant wristwatch with black figure sheet and black bracelet lay in the box. Warily I took out them; she admired of all sides and put on them. She has a ceramic bracelet and also the case of the clock was from ceramics. I ascertained a noble, very costly present and spoke:

»Nevertheless, something like that is expensive.«

»For it I work and for you nothing should be too expensive to me.«

Your words surprised me and I was concurrent enthusiastically about what you gave to me.

»I have never got a present which is so unique, as this. Thanks.«

Then we deeply looked in ourselves and with the magic sparkle of your sky-blue eyes you revealed to me your blessedness. Your luminous eyes were like a spark of the innocence, like a spark of the cleanness, a report to have found a little bit particularly. You caused a magic in me which I could not resist.

I had forgotten the Valentine's Day, an inexcusable fact which it was a matter to change now. Thus I called on the Monday morning my department in Hannover and pushed forward an authority visit to win time, to procure a suitable present fast still.

The nicest present what I can give you is still the sincerity and the honesty to be in heavy times with you and to stand always to you. However, you know this, believe I at least, so I had to surprise you still with additional presents.

Maybe I should cook sometimes, three ways menu from the microwave; a dear poem on cardboard write and to a jigsaw puzzle cut; a riddle provide with personal questions and the solution word proves the present, for example, a concert map, a great musical or a slip of paper box with 365 slips of paper, everybody with a special message, a dear wisdom.

If I had more time and lay of the Valentine's Day still weeks before myself, one could have realized many nice things.

However, actually, the bishop Valentin von Terni was a martyr who was executed on the 14th of February, 269 because he had dared a couple like a Christian, although at the time every Christian action was strictly forbidden. Only in the year 303 the Christianity was patient and 311 where proclaimed to state religion.

Valentin had given to the freshly married pairs of flowers from his garden and still today thus the custom is that most people buy bouquets preferentially to give away them. Besides, flowers have only one low life span of just spot one till two weeks.

Maybe I'd better give a spa and beauty experience. However, it can also be taken as a misinterpretation. I can already hear now your words: *I look about as ugly that I have to hide behind cucumber slices?* No, you need not really hide you.

Perfume! It is mostly kept in bottles which wake the impression of particularly a lot of contents, do not contain, however, unfortunately, sometimes half as a lot as they are big. Then the choice where one makes a distinction between thousands of different perfumes, everybody with different smell. Actually perfume is only a means to hide or to beautify the body odor.

But why sometimes in the Valentine's Day the darling with a short trip do not surprise? Simply search aim, suitcases pack and discover a new town.

I found the idea good and went to the travel agency, besides, thought of a weekend trip, thus from the next Friday till Sunday. The travel shop assistant suggested different aims to me:

Paris would be an absolute classic for lovers. A town in the famous poor Le mur des t'aime where love explanations were perpetuated into more than 300 languages.

Vienna, a visit in the St. Stephen's Cathedral, will to smell coffee in a traditional coffee house and a journey with the big dipper in the Prater.

Lisbon, den Torre de Belém, the landmark of the town with his many turrets and little windows, a romantic place for lovers.

Budapest, here you have hot spoiled for choice in about a hundred and twenty and twenty-one plunged impressive tradition baths of the city.

In Copenhagen, the bridge "Bryggebroen". Who attaches here a castle and throws the key in the river, love will hold lifelong.

Milan disposes of the most exclusive shopping street, Nice fascinates by his relative mild temperatures and in Rome one can proceed on the tracks of the saint Valentin, to the patron saint of the lovers.

»However, such excursions are already booked on weeks in advance,« reported the travel shop assistant. »Finally, the day after tomorrow Valentine's Day.«

»That is … nothing more freely?«

She shook the head and I sat there, still had no present.

»If it is about how they mentioned to be relaxing a few days, to be with her darlings sometimes completely only, maybe also far away of the civilization, then I could recommend them alternatively a house in Denmark. Indeed, the houses are rented week by week, from Saturday till Saturday.«

»OK, that is one would have to take a whole week from vacation. This also sounds well and Denmark is not far removed.«

»We have here,« spoke the travel shop assistant further, »houses directly on the beach, in the dunes, on natural properties, with pool, without pool, with Jacuzzi and sauna, without Jacuzzi and sauna, with fitness space, without fitness space, by the sea, in the wood.«

Quick I found an ideal house, booked for one week next month; it allowed to print out to me in the form of a voucher and went to you in the company.

I was excited like a small child, could hop about stretched umbrellas and make an estimate with the swing. I was stretched over your reaction to spend one week exclusively only with myself.

»I have here an envelope for you. The porter said, I should give him to you, but only you.«

You took the envelope and said:

»You swindler, we have no porter.«

»Oh what, then it was, well, your boss who acted so mysteriously, cryptic and enigmatically.«

You opened him and your face shone more nicely than ever. Carefully you looked at the voucher, at the description of the house, the property, the area and asked something irritated:

»Want you to excel me with your present? A week Denmark with you all alone?«

»Yes, actually, I had asked the lady in the travel agency, but it had no time. No, I want to show you only with the fact that it is serious to me. I would like to know like it is if we annoy ourselves the whole day.«

With a very intensive kiss you proved to me, that to have found right present. With pleasure I would have still remained, however, my job called me once again to Hannover.

One month later we went together in the vacation and it was a thrilling and nice vacation. I might experience wonderful days and it felt great to have you constantly around me. Our love blossomed in quite another shine.

And then were there still the moments at which all of a sudden a smile crept over your face because my thoughts had walked just to you. The moments which only we experienced two and understood. Mostly these were amusing circumstances which were cheerful and were let out; sometimes it was also a sentence of you which had engraved in my memory.

You were the woman who got to touch me with easy, simple words and you knew this because you knew me better than me myself. You were – and are – a part of my life and the other end of the bridge which connected our hearts with each other.

6. Love needs more, than just space

A nice time passed in which I could really experience you to hold you in the arm to feel that I might be I myself in your present and you as accepted me as I am; the fact that I could see in your eyes over and over again, how much you love me and which became clearer and clearer to me that you were the right thing.

It was Monday once more where I was on the move in the West German space, indeed, this time only up to Thursday, because on Friday a conference of my local office was fixed. So that it becomes a full success, such meetings are held outside from cities in villages with a rural kitschy ambience to create an optimum sphere in which one can concentrate to hundred percent upon the work-related problems and subjects.

The best, however, to such a meeting is the catering. Here no expense or effort is spared to convince the parties that you have chosen the right company. Buffet with pork loin skewers; Roasted turkey breast, mozzarella sticks, chili peppers filled with cream cheese; Spring rolls Vietnamese style, mini meatballs, mini schnitzel, pork medallions; Antipasti Vegetables, Roasted lamb chops, small chicken legs; Fried fish cubes, selection of fish fillets, shrimp, tomato mozzarella; Melon ham, marinated rump, Different salads of the season are not uncommon and convince high-spirited every time to attend such a meeting.

My mobile phone rang. I looked at the display; it was an SMS of you. You had never sent an SMS. Something must have happened, thought to me, worries and hoped for nothing bad. These are thus the moments where one sits thoughtfully there and thus a conference does not want to come to an end all at once because one believes that just now the leader gives his recitation in a very long-pulled viscous liquid speech of himself.

Actually, they work only for alibi reasons to be proved as a countermove to her luxuriant salary also sometimes as a teacher.

In the break I tried to call you several times, however, in vain, it was always taken. My worry rose and thus read I to me an excuse occur to stay away the other course of the conference. However, I did not want to renounce the sideboard and thus I got on the way only when the hunger was virtually satisfied.

Despite disregard every red light; I did not come forward faster. A construction site ensured that a line of cars was ideal living conditions. They block all-weather roads and so far you have only a few Ge-antidotes found to banish them from the road.

Rear-like the vehicles moving on, let me sniff the vapors of the above-propelled vehicles. But after some time reported traffic cone back down on an unobstructed road.

Quick the traffic found his normal state and the speedometer again his true speed could register.

Suddenly in front of me a vehicle of a driving school, based on the state road, at a rate of well below the pace of a play street, then creeps and slowly begins to provoke me. There are students; which is taught to focus on the steering wheel, in which case they forget the position of the accelerator pedal.

Slowly I crept behind the vehicle, had no chance to overtake him, because the counter track was frequented by strong traffic.

But just before reaching the city center, he turned happily from a side street and left me free ride. Already was the next problem to me. At one just cracked on green traffic light but actually chokes the front man from the engine of his car and gets him only to start again when the lights have long stood on red.

Now missing is the wrong-way driver, which is then followed by someone who wants to tell him that he goes in the wrong direction.

Then, finally, after an extensive competition in the urban motor sport, I stood before your door.

»Hey,« you shouted when the door rose.

»Hey, I have received your SMS, why does not go you to the phone what is wrong.«

I walked in, closed the door and went behind you. In one hand you would hold the phone, in the other hand a letter.

»You had said waiting loop with my lawyer,«. »I must depart here, the row houses in this street should be sold everybody.«

A little bit surprised, I asked in an absurd tone over again: »Ha-ha, your flat should be sold?«

»Do you find anyhow wittily?« you replied to me tomboyish.

»No, but I have received your SMS and thought …, we leave. What can I do?«

»You already do this, thanks that you have come.«

These were fireworks of the feelings again which shot by my body when you embraced me and you kissed me on my slightly open mouth.

»But, nevertheless, this is no problem,« then I mentioned, »I have simply told that my contact lenses have loose contact and, therefore, I would have to go home.«

»I have one month to search for myself a new flat, but hardly time for it. One of my colleagues has already offered his couch to me and with my parents I could also enter. But I do not surrender so easily. Either I defend myself or …«

»… or we move together,« I interrupted you.

You took the listener of the ear, lowered the arm and looked at me. Your blue eyes caught in to shine, sparkled all at once like diamonds; like the waves of a swimming pool whose surface were illuminated by the sun and your expression could suddenly tell stories.

You said only: »Wow« what I answered even with »Wow«.

Long time we were confronted silently and I saw in your eyes like you over and over again tried to realize my words. It seemed in such a way, as if you doubted them, as if you mistrusted me or had the even same doubts.

Suddenly all at once the other participant on the phone contacted: »Can I help them? Whom would like they to speak?«

Your eyes were still fixed on me when you took the listener to the ear and answered:

»Nobody, I have just decided to move together with my friend.« As a result you laid the listener again on the fork and came to me quite near. Admirable looks felt the faces and everybody it enjoyed to be devoured by the looks of the other.

Yes it was a decision which had to be well considered, because one surrenders a lot of his usual living spaces if one moves together.

Another everyday life! How will he look like? It is a conversion of the existing housing and living conditions, a sudden division of the premises.

How would you manage with the kink that I do not put my shoes in the shoe cupboard and that the dirty dishes land not in, but on the washer?

How we create mutual clearances, so that a living together does not become the tragedy.

Now, most time I spent the night at you. As for the rest we divided everything with each other what one can divide, and you endured my quirks up to now with a smile because you knew that one must simply accept certain things.

Actually, I could also fancy nothing nicer, than to wake every morning beside you and to fall asleep in the evening beside you; to go shopping at Aldi with every week, even if I do not feel like bumping into people whom one cannot suffer.

Now the first step is done, must put apart me with the new situation and tie off me from my single life.

Days later when I attended once again in Hannover space and was just on the way to a customer there rang my mobile phone.

»I have miraculous news,« you were in report. »I have found a flat for myself, in a smaller well cultivated arrangement.«

»Wow, this is great.«

»These are 3,5 room flats, not far from the town remotely, with pretty east Asian's broads grass wallpaper in the hall and cork walls in the sitting room.

»Oh what is really great, this,« I reacted easily irritated.

»Great in terms of fantastically or rather "in terms of me doubt has"?«

»I have no doubts, honestly not! The wish with you Together to move came from the deepest heart. I am covered at the moment with a lot of work, a little unfocused and I do not like grass wallpaper and cork walls to be quite honest.«

»In order I will continue to search if it is really the only reason.«

»There is no other reason, really not, believe me this.«

»And why do you hang then still on the phone? Hang up and go work!« you spoke in an imperious tone.

»Certainly, lady, will continue immediately,« I answered.

Thus you were and thus I have loved you. On the one hand a Little distrustfully, on the other hand quizzical and roguish. While I carried out my field service straight through Germany, you studied all newspaper and attacked thoughts which demands one should make to the new flat; finally, one spends there a large part of his life. To feel fine there, to be really at home, one of the most important criteria is with such a search. There are present the size and equipment, as well as the situation and traffic binding important points, as well as also the social sphere should fit.

Every evening we called up and you reported extensively about your efforts, about your negotiations and your thoughts as the new home will look if it should be furnished.

»A house with a garden, with four rooms, many cellars and a huge terrace,« you told beaming with joy when I was in the middle of the city highway Hanover again. »You want to look at the house with me?«

»Clearly, when?«

»Saturday! I hope that it till then has stopped to rain. You should see the house with sunshine.«

»Why, the roof is leaking? Or do bats live there?«

»Nonsense!«

»Or has the cellar become by the rain an experience outdoor swimming pool?«

» Be it out seriously, or do you want to pinch at the last moment?«

»No, I want to come along the house see, with or without bats, or without experience outdoor swimming pool.«

»Have you also thought seriously to move together with me?«

»Well logo, this I have and I want it!«

On Saturday it was dry, as well as you had wished it. We visited the house and it was really THE object. It was so big that comfortably two Households interrupted could become. Thus we signed the hire contract and also soon entered. My job disturbed me only one.

I was constant on move, goes over many town streets, country roads, federal routes, highways and if I leave the skin seaways, the civilization also disappeared more and more.

Then mostly one nowhere lands in, between a few scattered farms where supposedly representatives have sat down who aimed at a cooperation with my large-scale enterprise. If one lands in such areas, one assumes for the moment from the fact that the address cannot be right. However, then one finds these small tiny signs, embedded on a few silted up agriculture ways which point to a court which apparently belongs to a farmhouse.

»Yes, this is great that they have come. Would not have thought that they would find actual here.«

If the farmer who comes dressed with overalls and wellington just from a cowshed, welcomes to one with such words and embraces then so warmly that he presses almost the lungs from the neck calls then one such a sphere of activity a bad joke.

Already in the Stone Age the people were anxious to find animal cookers to guarantee the supper and a female cave woman to protect the future of the family.

Today it is not different much. The person was born to strive for his life aim, to work and to found a family, to build a house, to generate a child and a tree to plant.

7. A Message with Message in a bottle

For the next days I dealt in the north that was called, I was more regular than, otherwise, at home, mostly already at noon.

With certain attention or surprises, tries to show her to you over and over again that you were the most important person in my lives. I am glad about your smile when I had given either what to you, you surprised or simply allowed something.

Thus something was floating around to me once again in my head to hand over quite a personal message in a bottle on an unusual way to you.

Sun, water, vacation and living being would be the absolute ambience and so I remembered our beach on the Elbe, an ideal place for my project

So I fetched you directly at the work and spoke:

»Come lets us go for a walk on the Elbe.«

»But, nevertheless, I have no beach clothes with,« you contradicted.

»That does not matter, I also have nothing to do with. Or should I get you a red striped swimsuit with legs.«

»Ha, ha, ha,« I heard only.

We went under it to the beach, took off our shoes to feel barefooted the warm, soft, relaxation-worthy sand.

Easy stomping we crossed the bizarre and beautiful scenery of the shore strip, let the sand off our feet and take it in her sink into softness, which can attenuate the incidence and jumps cushioned. With each step I felt the small-grained sand between your toes trickled as easy feet massaged, tickled, almost caressing. It was like the feeling of a soul massage.

A stripe with square, broken rock rubbish was fastened directly to the water, an elevation for the protection of the waters shoulder. Between the stones sloshed over and over again the small waves up which searched her way back in the river, a good place for my message in a bottle.

The bottle has a long history. They used to call for help as pirates services, to draw attention to their plight at sea. Later it was even made to science, to send messages to their homeland. Today, it would be an alternative to the social networks to make friends around the world.

First I wanted to send together with you a message in a bottle and bind the handing over of the message in a bottle to the mood of the river. The image where the trip could go for the bottle and together with you tuned me joyfully.

Then the idea you came to me in similar manner to surprise at home, to leave my message in a bottle in the bath if you were just taking a bath. However, you would note immediately who is behind this action and thus I decided on the variation that you the "by chance" found pirate's news fishes even from the water.

The beach was almost empty. Some couples were in the sand and were irradiated by the sun; others hurled flat stones across the water so that they often possible jumped over the water surface before they sank. Lovers were entwined along the shore, and some stopped, looked at the water, where just one of those huge container ships the Elbe went along.

Certainly, as the luxury liner Queen Mary 2 impressive, but the largest ships arriving in Hamburg, times are now container ships. There are ships with a length of almost four hundred meters and a width of fifty meters. They are the true giants of the Port of Hamburg.

The sand invited to give us, so we put ourselves down and let our bodies from the sun heat. Quietly, I hear the sound of the waves, which rubbed against the rock boulders. About the seagulls cried, standing effortlessly as though glued to the sky and look out for what kept edible.

In the distance I see two boys holding a plate-shaped Frisbee alternately tossed to and fro. A popular, trendy leisure and beach-toy that is easy to handle. By throwing the disc rotates top-shaped and holds thereby in the air and in his flight path.

I look to you under it, your eyes were closed, you had deeply sunk into thoughts which swarmed round you and lent you an eager expression. I sneaked away quite quietly, ran to the car and got the bottle, as well as a tray, covered with a bell-sharped lid under which a small snack was.

I stowed away the message in a bottle quite near to the water, stuck between two stone stones, so that it is not carried away immediately by the smallest wave.

Then I crept back, laid me beside you and listened to your breath. You pushed you air from the lungs and inhaled them again, again out and after the motto, I have still forgotten what, you fetched back them again.

A shade fell on your face when I bent over you. Slowly you opened your eyelids and I saw the warm shine of your sky-blue eyes.

»I have procured what to food for myself,« I spoke and removed, besides, the lid.

A pineapple appeared, equipped with limited toothpicks on which in each case a piece of cheese, alternately with white and blue bunches of grapes were, as well as with tangerines and small cherry tomatoes.

At the front end a smooth cut, before it a rectangular disc of pineapple, at the head a grape as a nose and in the middle two as eyes.

»However, this is dear from you, have you made this same? Looks like a mouse …, your cheese hedgehog.«

»Well, as five stones cook, I can heat up not only courts up to the blistering, but also produce cheese hedgehog with the appearance of a mouse.«

We fed ourselves mutually and when the hedgehog had strongly lost in weight, it became a time to realize my plan.

»Come, let us on the shore a little stone can jump over the water, let's see who is better.«

»I am better,« you answered, jumped up, gave me a kiss on the mouth and went slowly in the direction of shore. While I still stowed away fast our utensils in a bag, I shouted to you behind:

»No you are not, on which you recalled indignantly:

»Am I that!«

»No!«

»Yes!«

»OK,« I spoke when I had caught up you. »Whose stone hops first 8 spot about the water, has won.«

»OK.«

Like small children we behaved, this was always in such a way when we were together. You will never become adult and beside you I also remained a child.

Me collected on the way already nice level stones; gave to you some and knocking going on. The first ones sank immediately into the water, however, then you also got the trick out to throw the stones properly and always on occasion they bounced off of the water surface.

Slowly I moved towards bottle, trying to lure you add there what you made also unnoticed. Then there came the throw which assured of the first place in this duel me. About 8 spot the stone of the water surface bounced off, before he set finally. Joyfully I swayed in the hips and started to swing with the head rhythmically, wanted to offer you thus my victory.

However, no admirable words were to be heard from you, no common one sniff in the smell of the success, no common jumping on the steps of the recognition, to no common spoons from the winner's trophy, only one amazed:

»Did not think that someone can be so very pleased with the stone hopping.«

»This says a woman who has got just to sink the stone four times about the water.«

»5 spot,« was your objection. »5 spot.«

»However, fight mind I may,«

»I know,« you answered.

With gentle force I pulled you up to me, hugged you tight and a gentle breath hit my cheek. Security enveloped me, mediated affection and warmth. A moment that would forever so can stay.

Affectionately you looked at me, laid your head on my shoulder and I felt how your luck spread to me. Narrow embraced we looked at water, observed the ferries which went straight across the Elbe to carry people of a landing stage to the others.

»I interrupted show sometimes a bottle,« our contemplation. »There even a slip of paper is in it, a message in a bottle determines.«

»You believe that it is the cry for help of a castaway here on the Elbe?«

»Ha, ha, not determined. It is rather the news of a research team of Antarctic. Give me your hand, I hold on you and you get them.«

I held up my hand firmly, it went into a crouch and let you climb the stones down. Far and wide were no crowds and heavy-lift, and no container ships to see the bow waves could pile up to the shore.

Actually, I did not need to hold on you, because the bank edge cultivation went with extremely level inclination to the water. It was only to give you the feeling that you could weigh yourself in security. Moreover, it lay to me in the heart that you got the bottle, because, finally, it was determined also for you.

»There a slip of paper really is in it,« you noted when you had again "firm ground" under the feet.

»Open sometimes and read what stands on it.«

»You mean, one can open the bottle so simply?«

»Does a name stand there somewhere in it or an address?«

You looked to you the bottle of all sides and meant:

»No.«

»Then you can open the bottle quietly.«

It was a small transparent a little thicker bottle, closed with a wide cork which rose half of it out. The slip of paper was tied together with a booklet, so that he could glide like a tube from the bottle. You rolled out the paper and spoke:

»You, who have the same name us me.«

»R-e-a-l,« I acted surprised, »this is a thing.«

»Yes really, look here.« You moved with your forefinger at the name along and caught to the first lines silently before yourself to read.

»Wow, then« I heard. »This is a love letter. Sound sometimes,« and already you started citing the letter loudly:

…says my look how much I loves you how unfathomably happily you make me and that I would never again like to give you. Words like love, trust and luck do not come roughly at what I feel for you if you stand before me and take me in the arms.

I do not feel so probably in your present, how for a long time any more. How could I have been so long exist without you, without your closeness and warmth that I'm so good! I wish from whole hearts that there remains always so.

Nothing will create it, that to split tape which has connected our hearts. And if it should try, nevertheless, once somebody, I will prevent it with all means.

I love you!

Tears rolled all at once in your cheeks down which I could not interpret first. If these were emotional tears those of the lines were due or tears of the luck because you knew from which the letter came. I took you in the arms, pressed you quite firmly to myself and listened to your sobbing. Affectionately you read your hand about my back glide and a magnificent phenomenal feeling originated what was thrilling and erotizing.

»Darling,« I heard after a while.

»Yes.«

»Nevertheless, he is from you. Why do you make something like that with me?«

»So that you know what I feel for you.«

»Nevertheless, I know this.«

» Yes, but you should get to know it again and again.«

»You're killing me over and over again at a loss if you come up with these ideas. How can I ensure only show gratitude?«

»With a romantic dinner on the roof of a hotel, perhaps?«

»Oh, you're stupid,« you had answered it, though I had meant it with the food on the roof of a hotel.

8. Money cannot by happiness

In the meantime I acted already more than two weeks in the metropolitan area Hamburg and anyhow I liked it to come home every day and together with you, to be relaxing in our own four walls. Sometimes we went out and sometimes we lay even together on the sofa, watched TV or chatted.

One day I got the order in Frankfurt to deliver a lecture on the sea place Hamburg and indeed before many colleagues.

»What should be reached with the talk,« it interested me.

»Formulate him in such a way that it becomes exciting for the other listeners.«

»Should I report a crime film or a seminar paper?«

»You already know what I mean, briefly and expressively.«

»Which technologies stand to me at possession? Overhead projector, video projector or flipchart?«

»This remains to them leave. It is important that they point out the people to it at which works they can earn a lot of money and where they pay extra constantly.«

»Excuse me, I thought, I should hold a talk on the sea place Hamburg and provide no analysis.«

»The one you can combine well with the others when they do the skill.«

»Yes, however, I am not the superior of the listeners that of my opinion it is incumbent only upon the managers.«

»If they think of her future, the company still plans a lot with them,« I got to hear. »Sometime they will sit on this chair here and this is why it is not so bad at all sometimes if they take by now a certain initiative.«

And the submissive conversation very flighty for me was finished with it all of a sudden.

Because after the talk one more conversation was planned which should give explanation about my other activity within the group, this "initiative" was probably an aspect for my bosses, however, not for me.

Earlier it had made no difference to me to do me the whole week in other metropolises, pleased me even to get to know new towns and villages, to cost kitchens specific for region, to meet with other mentalities.

But today, when I experience the beginning of a relationship, of which I have always dreamed of, it's different. I have to leave no more like our home for days.

Every time I have the essence that is closest to me, always leave and after I learned you just met. One week, five working days, usually go quickly around. But I currently come one day before like a year and five days like an eternity.

I missed you very much and this permanent longing limited my quality of life terrifically. We experienced two different everyday realities and could not divide a lot with each other. During the week I am associated myself single and on the week-end.

The oldest and strongest feeling is the fear, the oldest and strongest form of the fear, is the fear of the stranger, before the future.

What is if we drifted apart and we developed in different directions, only because I am so seldom at home? Of course such "a weekend respect" has his advantages, one receives the magic of the being fresh-in love over and over again. The fear remains still continue to exist to be able to lose something like you.

Sometimes I sit in my hotel room and would reach at this moment simply with pleasure for you to take you in the arm. You push me to feel your skin and get involved with every fiber of my body on you.

However, you are not there and everything what I can act is to think of you. So I had asked already some time ago my bosses to limit my job to the metropolitan area Hamburg, because the common time with you is too valuable to waste them and telephone calls are comparable with your presence in no manner.

Thus I was stretched on the conversation and on the result that will get quite a new value. Joy climbed up in me, like at that time when I became fully-fledged and left the parental home. To me my first flat furnished and pushed the first pizza in the oven.

The next days I prepared for my talk, expected by an enthusiastic appearance and a good search to score and to find an attentive audience.

»And when you are there again,« you ask and I felt this light longing undertone which you always had when I prepared for my departure.

»Well, on Monday journey and common dinner with colleagues and on Tuesday is this talk. Then I remain one more night because I have on the Wednesday morning one more discussion with the executives. Then I will see that I take the direct way home. So between evening and midnight I am fine again here. Why do you ask?«

»Oh it is always absent what when you are not there. Often I wake up in the middle of the sleep and must think of you.«

»I know, my treasure,« replied I. »I know.«

»Where from do you know this?«

»Because I just feel, how you.«

On time I was on the highway, stopped in Hannover to take my acting department manager there. For his return journey he had to come to an arrangement with another colleague. On the way we made in a motorway service area just around a snack ourselves to take.

It was a marvelous day which radiated the sun and a warm summer feeling appeared. In low distance I see the clouds which have the appearance of a herd of meek sheep. An airplane flies through and shines in the sun like a silver arrow.

I took off my sports jacket and laid it in the boot to protect it against thieving eyes. My colleague did the same one. In the outside area we took a seat and ordered what to food.

Suddenly it occurred to me that my car key was in the sports jacket, the sports jacket in the trunk lies and the trunk was closed.

»Shit, my car key is in the trunk.«

»Oh, this is not so good,« I agreed as an answer. »What is with the second key?«

»Hey?,« I noted surprised. »The question was quite absolutely superfluous, or do you always have a spare key, besides, maybe in the heel of your shoe or in the sock?«

»No that is not. But there are some, they have attached small hiding places in the bumpers to bend forward such topic.«

Is right, there he was already right. There are many people such hiding places have. Particularly surfers hide her keys always in the car, somewhere in the tire, in the grill or in the bumper, before they rush in the floods.

However, with the today's construction method would be with a bumper hiding place, the complete dismantling of those inevitably.

I considered how one could open such a car fastest and easiest one without causing sensation and without being surprised by a hard armed special force of the police which chains one after an extensive body search with handcuffs and keeps under lock and key for days in pretrial detention.

»Maybe I should smash one of the rear side discs and open thus the vehicle.«

»I believe, the probably most favorable possibility would be to call yellow Angel. They know a lot about something like that.« if meant my colleague.

No bad thought and how the chance it in such a way wants, I saw just driving one of these yellow mobile garages on the parking bay. A man with waving hands shut to him and piloted him to his vehicle. I shut on with a banana-yellow overall with silver reflex stripes dressed man, described my mishap to him and allowed to put off myself about a few minutes.

During the waiting, I observe three only ten-year-old boys on a bank, with canned beer and cigarettes. Besides, my youth occurred to me, had smoked my first cigarette with fourteen to maltreat with the girl's impression. However, then was so dizzy to me that I the feeling had the whole world would turn on me, as if I made an ass bomb of the three with 180 ° rotation.

Today the kids are case-hardened and start earlier and earlier with the smoking. While at my time still baby monitor stood in the children's rooms, today smoke dispatch riders hang on the covers.

I had taken alcohol only with sixteen to myself when my cousin bottled me on a celebration with the good old Oldesloer. I was drunk after three glasses in such a way which I like an epileptic started to dance and me, besides tried to ram into the ground. My food came on reverse way again outside and landed on the shirt of my uncle what was a light aim, because he stood just before me. Surprised I looked at the mushy mass which still looked completely different to food. As a result I landed first with the head under the cold shower and then with wet hair in the bed.

Today the kids drink because they believe to look thereby emancipated and adult.

After fairly long time the mechanic came to us and asked again for the circumstances.

»In order for our jackets not as visible around the car as we had stowed in the trunk. Besides, I had not remembered that the vehicle key was still in my jacket. Well and now we stand there and should be, actually, long time ago in Frankfurt.«

»No problem, they can go on at five minutes. I will spread the door a little and then solve with a wire latch. Then the trunk would have to allow opening also,« explained the man of the yellow club.

With adhesive tape he protects before the door and he stretched the roof before damages and with a silicone-like wedge the door frames of the car body. An aerial cushion distinguished the gap consistently and thus he could penetrate with a wire into the vehicle inside. Promptly I also heard the noises of the central locking which unlocked all doors.

Contently about this service which had lasted really no longer as five minutes and might welcome at the same time me as a new member we got out our sports jackets and went on.

After a good two hours we already saw the mighty skyscrapers of the resident banks, assurances and other financial service companies. To find the way to the hotel was a light, because the description by the secretariat was very specific.

The evening ran quite apathetically, tiring and deadly boring. One sat with like-minded colleagues together, spoke of women, tractors and of the seminar paper to be held tomorrow.

All the time I asked myself how such half-clever could be appointed executives to show off tried with specialist knowledge, but in the final effect only superlative know-it-alls are. Objections such as

»What one should still disregard, besides, in this connection …« or

»Basically it is so right, indeed …,« or

»And one must mention, nevertheless…,« were no rarity, however, none of itself could give reasonable arguments or also views.

Even if we live in a democracy, this is not called that every level pear can join in the conversation, already not at all if one to the opinion is to be owned a lot of specialist knowledge and still only shit talks.

I rather went on my room and had called you because I had the need to hear your affectionate voice in my ear.

»I repeated everything only level pears, and imitated then one of the colleagues: »Though I have no notion of the subject, but it should be reworked.«

»Do not get excited, Darling, otherwise you still get grey hair.«

»At the moment my pulse is only in the terrible one knock and my heart in race. If just a self-diagnosis has carried out and has said them that it does not look well for me.«

»Oh of poor Darling, how I can help you?«

»Humph …, maybe with a common soft evening.«

»Then must see you that you come here as soon as possible. So come along on the socks.«

» If I would make me now on the socks, then I would not be before tomorrow evening at home, so I'm here only times my job and then go out of convenience rather drive home. OK?«

»If somebody has already said you that you bit silly,« you asked.

»Yes, you some days ago,« I replied.

You got that over and over again to bring me for smiling, even if to me was one second before still absolutely sickening. I do not know how you make this, but I am glad that you make it and I would like to miss it by no means.

The next day I held my seminar paper before 200 field representatives and noted that not only intelligence allergy sufferers were present like which from yesterday, but also eager, participant and itself interests showing ones. In the next two talks, one revealed that my talk was like a dialogue, like a dialogue between the single listeners and me, essentially in the engaged conversational tone

A positive day which strengthened my confidence even more and confident look ahead to tomorrow's interview revealed.

The working hours of most managers does not begin before ten o'clock and thus my discussion had been also fixed only for this time.

I was asked in one of these very magnificently furnished offices of the managers. A room that was so big that you had to run a few times steps to reach the desk of the manager.

A run distance with the underlining meaning which is comparable with the way to the throne in a king's hall. Then partially still the visitor's chairs were shortened by some centimeters what never became conscious by one, to the opponent, nevertheless, a certain dominance lent.

On the sides everywhere bushy plants in extravagantly made vessels from hand-twisted hemp. In between massive busts on stony columns, an elegant attribute for the office of a great breadwinner.

Pieces of furniture from noble materials, with perfect design and in top implementation carry the wish for individuality and quality for calculation. Games like in the desk intrigued, cooled drink bars; the televisions which disappear with a TV lift from the view field and a video projector sunk in the conference table let arise luxury feeling in the office everyday life.

I sat down before the desk and admired the picture in the back of my manager sitting opposite me. However, a piece of art, molder in the abstract and absolutely very expensive.

The second manager came and without long prefaces one praised me in the highest tones, spoke nice words, flattered and smeared me by the kilo honey around the mouth that it dripped only so. Then the other took over the word:

»At the beginning of every top achievement stands always the readiness to be involved in the highest measure of an aim. Since on the wish the skill – and then follows mostly also step by step at the end the reward.«

I was with the thoughts, already on the return journey, hoped that I do not get in some traffic jam and considered with what I could surprise you sometimes. However, then I was suddenly torn from my thoughts when I suddenly heard somewhat from a move.

»I have not understood Excuse me, this completely. Could they repeat this again?«

»Who of his employees heroic deeds desirably, must also be able to bring considerations. We would welcome it, therefore if they could resolve to move her domicile in the space Hannover.«

»That is I should move if I interpret this properly. However, I had asked for a field of application in Hamburg.«

»Every person who performs tallness also wishes that his achievements are recognized and are esteemed. Besides, we do not expect that they move to Frankfurt. We offer them a new field of application which applies over Niedersachsen and Bremen to Hamburg.«

»This is nice, but my family lives in Hamburg and also my friend with whom I have moved together scarcely, lives there. I do not want to break what was built up just so sensitively, therefore, also my request to limit my activity to a regional levels.«

»You are one of our best and most successful employees and I pronounce this praise not only from nothing but desire and love, no it should act for them like a signpost on the street to the success.«

»I must think about it first,« I mentioned to finish this conversation that in no manner only one fraction of my request considered.

»You must not decide immediately. Think again about it. If they note, however, please that there is an essential step on the steps of the career leaders also for them. Then their sphere of activity applies from Göttingen to Hamburg and it immense financial advantages will come up to them.«

»Thanks, but only money does not make not happily, at least me.«

»We would take over even the costs of the move, put to them a company vehicle at possession which they could also use privately.«

»It is not about material things, it is about my psyche, about my most tender wish, around my emotional life.«

»All understandable, but if it were my son, I would advise them to their new area of responsibility. If they sleep quietly about that, then we speak to us over again. We would really regret it if we lost such a capable employee, our hope lies only with them.«

Shortly after I was again on the highway, wanted just home. I let pass everything once more revue. Only this mucus run, how well and how great one is and then the gun is put to one on the breast, hop or top. If I do not accept the new challenge, tomorrow I am jobless; if I accept them, however, by now I know that I will lose you and this lies to me far.

However, hardly I left the smoked pork mountains behind myself, my decision was certain. I work in a noble section and there are only a few which have entirely learnt this activity and can exercise. Thus there will be for me also no difficulty to find a new job in the same or similar section.

Late in the evening I came home and you received me, as if I had been on the move months.

»How was your trip?« you asked.

»Well, so-so. My talk has completely arrived safely, the very much interested people with whom one could exchange himself in this subject were also present up to the nerds of the day before.«

»What I can do then good for you,« you asked with an extremely enticing voice what I answered only briefly:

»Tasty food and a massage!«

9. A romantic atmosphere

I had told you up to now about my professionally planned change still nothing, wanted to surprise you in an adequate atmosphere with it, however, it ran differently than planned. Still I was tuned gladly to inform you of my decision which I had already like during the journey.

However, it should run not by necessity in a coexistence-seated conversation, but receive an unusual frame, finally, it was a decision which had cost a lot of overcoming and thus I called for the moment my old friend Ernie. He is a chauffeur of a well-heeled lady, lives in a separate small house on the property of his boss and deals at the moment nothing else, than to polish daily their Daimler.

»Hey Ernie, say sometimes your boss, nevertheless, is on vacation, or?«

»Is the next fourteen days still in Sweden with her family. Why do you ask?«

»I want to surprise my treasure with news and in addition I would need a certain ambience, a romantic atmosphere, idyllic surroundings where sea, candles, moon and the majestically setting sun becomes present if you know what I mean.«

Break entered and I noted like Ernie started to consider how he thought how he thought to himself. One properly heard the click of the gearwheels in his head if the teeth slowly adapted themselves in the gaps of the counter wheel. However, then all at once the spontaneous statement:

»Oh you mean Bali bed there below on the beach, the sun bench. Shure you can use the. When then?«

»Saturday I had thought if it goes. I want to organize there a small shred hunt.«

»Why you have lost what?«

»No I have lost nothing. It is not such a hunt like you know them, it is an area play. One lays out tips which one should follow to achieve an aim and in this case the tips should lead under it to the beach where I wait then.«

»You with your games, sometimes I have the feeling, you spin.«

»Thanks, nevertheless, I also love.«

It came Saturday and I can be fetched early in the afternoon by Ernie. We plan what all-important to do, I lied you, because I had to arrange still some preparations.

At the entrance I put an empty basket there with the tip that you had to do to take him. On the long entrance way to the villa I placed directly before the rose patch well obviously a bottle of champagnes, with a stuck begging comic figure and a speech bubble stood in that: Take me, take me.

Shortly before the villa I let two glasses on a big cloth stay and a slip of paper with the saying: Champagnes and sparkling wine tulips = a quiet-full sensory sensation.

At the side of the house in the middle on the way rested a red rose with the tip: for the favorite person in the world.

Then on the following lawn a bowl with strawberries gaudy red and for biting into sweetly, in the other course a dished plate with delightful chocolate sauce to dip, afterwards a plate with cut open kiwis and in the following a small little glass honey for the small, round, green fruit.

Shortly before the slope I caught to the way to under it to the beach with tea lights to create small light accents. These level candles in aluminum vessels create a romantic road company. Round the beach bed I put up with oil full torches.

The dusk entered and it became a time to call you and after a boozer-German dialect:

»Gooood day … everybody to-to-together.«

»Hello Darling. Say sometimes you have drunk?«

»What is? Hick um?«

»Whether you have drunk what,« I have asked you. »You are full.«

»No i-hick-dea, have o-o-nly two or so drinking beer. Can y-o-o-u-u-u pick me up?«

Behind me Ernie stood, listened in to the conversation, caught in to grunt and dropped crashing to ground.

»What was that,« you ascertained immediately. »Have you done to yourself what?«

»Ho-o-o-w would I k-n-o-w because.«

»This sounded, as if you had fallen down.«

»Uffa, which is a wind today. Can barely stand.«

»I believe, it is better if I get on the way immediately. I am with you in ten minutes.«

»She immediately goes past,« I spoke to Ernie who still lay on the ground and could not keep before laughter any more.

After him itself bit by bit calm had, he got up and disappeared, everlasting I lay down outstretched on the couch.

It is a double couch with white water-unfriendly and dirty-unfriendly relations, four posts with tied together curtains and a material-related baldachin as a solar protection. Sunk in the head part, a radio with auto-changer from which a pleasant one and the mood useful music sounded.

I looked for some time at the Elbe, at the ships going to and fro; on the big ones which must be towed by tractor to the mooring and on the small without impulse ones which are moved by tugboats.

Then, finally, with the full basket you got slowly closer and I saw a sensuous smile in your face. In big expectation to be able to close you immediately in my arms you got always closer.

Then you stood before me and I saw how a tear about your cheek rolled, a tear of the joy, the love, the security. I caught them with the forefinger and kissed the humid eyelids.

»Darling what you make with me,« you asked.

»Nothing my treasure, I only want to point you, how much you mean to me, point you as importantly you to me is. I want to say with the fact that I always want to listen to you when you need it; with you talk if you it wishes; think of you if you admit it. I always want to be there for you because I love you.«

You kissed me and when you gave up me, you deeply looked into me. At such moments our eyes illuminated themselves and we know both about that word of the love not only were simply said without thinking. Words are sometimes also absolutely superfluous; finally, one can also be quiet together with each other. Then I took from you the basket and spoke:

»What you have brought then there everything,«

»Oh, this lay around there everything thus in the middle of the way,« you had answered. »And because a name nowhere stood on it, there I have simply taken it. But why this expenditure what you plan and how you come on such idea?«

»Actually, I would have a lot more ideas. First I wanted to make a balloon ride with you, but you fly reluctantly. Then I thought in an overnight stay in the igloo; a Candle Light dinner in the prison; spaghetti ice eats in a Turkish bath; the visit of a Voodoo shaman who can celebrate curses with small figures from bone. However, all that was not substantial enough for you, so that I decided on this kind of a date. I have to inform you because of something what could maybe prepare a little friend for you. But before we drink a glass of champagne.«

I opened the fastener of the champagne bottle and sent the cork with one according to banging plopping on the way. However, by the high pressure which had been based in the bottle the champagne also shot like Fontaine from the bottle and landed on my trousers. Quick I still poured splashing the glasses with the sparkling champagne completely, before I started to complain about my appearance:

»Great, now I look as if I had peed in the trousers and, besides, I have only these trousers with.«

I looked at you without understanding and noted the expression in your eyes which hid an unrestrained cheek. You caught in to grin and squinted a little to side. Your mouth went out of shape to narrow lips and let arise small dimples in the cheeks.

And then it broke about you, you caught in dreadfully to laughter. Salvo-like you had pushed the breath out, your eyes became humid and after a while you kept the belly because slowly the diaphragm started hurting you.

It was one of these moments again where I could not simply think that you are an adult person. On the other hand, however, this naivety pleased me, this freshness you emitted and it released a well-being and a comfort in me.

When the laughter died down, you spoke:

»Not be sad, my treasure.«

Besides, you stroked at the same time my wet trousers, it started to stick at all places. An unpleasant feeling!

»You must not always be immediately so abusively and disdainfully to me if such a mishap happens to me sometimes.«

»But, nevertheless, you know Darling: who has the damage, does not need to provide for the mockery.« Besides, you grinned again in such a way, as if another storm flood of the laughter pounced on you.

»I look like a wet flour bag,« I ascertained embarrassingly on which you replied to me:

»Nevertheless, you can draw trousers of Ernie if it disturbs you.«

»Hello. Where I do drag the pants because? Ernie's clothes are ironed onto the driveway.«

»Ey maiden, do not act in such a way, or most sluggishly you recently skirts.«

»Yes, however, look, nevertheless, sometimes. This looks like aquaplaning at the highest level.«

You had held your level hand before my mouth, had forbade to talk to me with it further. Then your soft hands surrounded my face and you approached my mouth. Softly and affectionately our lips touched and a warmth full in a fairytale world, affection and passion rose.

»OK,« I said in the connection, »only canoe tours without capsizing.«

I took our both glasses and observed for some time how the small vesicles climbed up in the glasses as they worked reassuringly on me and a good mood sparkled.

Then we toasted to us, lay down on this colossal bed and I fed you on strawberries, dipped in aromatic sauce of milk chocolate, as well as with kiwis, covered with a light breath by honey.

»Thus it could be every day,« you swarmed.

»Every day?«

»Yes, every day.«

»What could be thus every day,« I asked.

»To be fed by you.«

»Oh you mostly, you lie here on a Roman food couch and allow feed yourself from a slave.«

» Y-e-s, exemplary and admirable idea, but unfortunately you're not at home every day.«

»By the way at home, I have to inform you still of what.«

»Then open fire sometimes, do not stretch me too much on the torture« you answered.

»If you can still remember the day where I had in the morning a meeting? It was no internal discussion, rather a concern for my part. It was about the fact that I had expressed the wish to limit my operational area to Hamburg. Yesterday I had the conversation with the upper bosses and this ran differently than expected.«

A little bit amazed you looked at me, considered only and then tried to guess the salient point. Quite carefully, with hardly audible voice you asked:

»Once … you … quiet … you?«

»No this not. It was only one conversation because of a transfer.«

»You do not want to go any more on travelling? Quite normal working days experience and every day at home are?«

»Thus I had planned it. From the Hamburg office it would have been no problem, only the managers from Frankfurt would see it a little bit different. For example, that I move, t not to Frankfurt but to Hannover. All costs to me from it originate, if one took over. One makes available even a company vehicle to me which I could also use privately and my chances to earn money would further affect to my advantage.«

Your face went out of shape, became sad and let arise small little folds between the eyebrows. The look was lowered, the eyes were half closed and the corners of mouth pointed far down. Then you spoke with melancholy depressed voice:

»That is you will move?«

I saw desperation in your face, a deep dismay with a pain. You became sad because something what was to you threatens to fail importantly; because I had disappointed you possibly; asks yourself, why the common flat when, nevertheless, I leave you now. You are deeply injured internally, see everything only in somber colors and can be glad about nothing more.

Your head was still lowered, was near the tears, fell in a deep hole and everything this agreed with my decision to turn the back towards the current company.

»If all that clapped so, this would be great for you,« you further spoke to me.» I wish you a lot of success, in your new surroundings.«

I took a strawberry, dipped them in the chocolate sauce and wanted that you bite off them. However, with inclined head you declined, simply had no more interest in such little plays. A gesture they were meant: leave me alone.

Who acts, however, in the field service, three "knows Hey it", *polite stubbornness helps* and because I knew, that Fortuna becomes immediately again smile, I still played a little with the fire.

»Bite off, nevertheless, please once, so that I can further continue with my implementation.«

»What you still want to tell how nice Hannover is that we could maybe see ourselves every few week-ends sometimes that I can visit you also sometimes or which is better it if we separated immediately.«

»No this not, but Hannover is really nice, the mansions garden, the Maschsee, the colorfully illuminated benches, the Old Town.

However, you know …, I had thought a lot as me Frankfurt had left …, to our respect which is for me something special …, recognizing your close soul …, the understanding from the outset …, to lose, besides the thoughts which we exchanged without word. Seldom a person had as come close to me as you …, and when I somewhere between Kassel and Göttingen was …, I knew …,«

Stroking I went over your head and your cheek, your chin raised with stooped forefinger, so that we saw what happen to us in the eyes and spoke:

»… there I knew that to us nothing could separate in the world, not sometimes thus a tempting position, how in Hannover. My decision is certain, I stay here. Monday I will announce my decision and search for myself here a new job. Probably one will give time off me first up to the end of the term of notice with full relations, but this makes nothing, is like paid-up vacation and then I would have time for myself what the fitting to search.«

Slowly you understood the situation, your misjudgment and a face with the nicest eyes and the nicest smile of the world noted spread out. I saw the luck in you that joy emitted to remain combined now, nevertheless, with your love.

You started to stutter: »Y-y-you s-s-stay? No l-l-longer going in the f-f-field?«

»In the field service maybe, but not in such a way that I must spend the night outwards, maybe one, twice, but not regularly.«

I still held out the strawberry in the hand, passed them to you again and quickly you had bitten off the strawberry up to the sepals.

It was nice to see again your beaming face, warmhearted, happily and playful. These were these moments again at which our looks met and united in quiet arrangement our thoughts.

»You will always remain with me,« you asked. »Promised?«

»Yes, Promised!«

You asked for fairly long time:

»And what do you still hide thus everything before me?«

»Nothing.«

»I do not believe this you, come tell.«

»Well, as a child I climbed with pleasure

quite high trees and I found swaying the branches under my feet as a special kick. One day I did not want any more under it and as a result my mother got the fire brigade.«

»Why did you not want there any more under it?«

»Because the view from was as nice up there, … just as now.«

Besides, I looked at you, saw in your narrow face with the big eyes and the elegant nose. Your eyelashes and eyebrows were emphasized by the dark contouring especially nicely.

»And what for secrets you have to hide in such a way,« I asked.

»Humph, with seven I puffed with pleasure soap bubbles, small and gigantic and if I succeeded a ball on my hand in letting float without which she burst, then I wished to be a bird to me always, to be able to fly and to see the world from another perspective.«

»No, I my no desirable image, I mine thus a right secret.«

»Oh you mean something hidden, a right secret,« you had answered. »I believe everybody something like that has, but I will not tell you mine.«

»How does one live then with such a secret?« I further asked to draw it out of you.

»Not well, something like that can eat up properly. Then it gnaws in like a bad illness. One gets feelings of guilt and the urge to let out the secret with all the strength, also whom one knows about that one can go in it to reason.«

It became quiet for seconds. Nobody is able to say just one word. I looked at you and felt like you sound out secrets of news. However, mostly I could assume from the fact that you let out your secrets at the speed of a flu virus.

»Why you ask? Until you already in this stage?« you interrupted my river of thought.

»No, no, no, this was only one lofty question. This deals nothing with you or us, is meant only so worldwide.«

»Oh, you are still in the phase where to one the feelings of guilt torment,« you tried to talk me.

»If you point sometime you do not endure it then any more, it does you in the insanity, you let out your secret and notice only then how it releases you.«

»Really?«

»Yes. Besides, of course you also are able to do your family, your friends maybe also your job lose, completely it comes on the secret on it.«

Yes so you were, self-confidently and critically and sometimes you simply do not read to yourself the reins from the hand take, as well as today.

It was a sensuous evening, the sun has already set since longer time and the moon has taken over the lighting. The subdued flickering garden torches demonstrated the champagne amber-colorfully.

Your blue eyes shone in the light of the fire and your face shone in a special personality. You were wonderful, with no model in the world comparably.

Together we looked at the water, the ships which swung cheerfully to and fro observed. An ocean-going ship loaded with container, into which were incredible amounts of incredible things, sailed along the Elbe.

On the other side of this waterway, the illuminated skyline of a terminal with huge, oversized loading units on rail transport systems. Here containers are continuously turned over from ship to truck and / or train or ship to ship.

A ferry crosses the Elbe. She was earlier with her cheeping warning tone and him howl of the machines one of the most important connections in the passenger traffic, while she brought shy people, accommodation people, Tally Men and Skipper to the single jetties of the ships. Today the ferries are to be thrown predominantly a maritime atmosphere for tourists around a look in the harbor docks to come close to the thick pots and to let swing on the waves of the Elbe.

Over us the stars, he is the garden of heaven. They are wonderful, particularly when one recognizes the star pictures.

»There you see, the big carriage,« you said.

»Yes, he is always good to recognize, by seven brightest stars.«

It was nicely to be admired this evening starry sky, especially impressively many small light-emitting diodes which look, as if luminous beetles send out signals.

»And where is now the Pole Star?« you asked when I had got involved just so properly in the world of the natural phenomena.

»Humph … if one connects both bright rear star points of the big carriage with each other and extends this line upwards by the fivefold one reaches more or less to the Pole Star.«

»And where is this approximate?«

I took your forefinger, held him in the air in such a way as if I glided over a star atlas, walked from the rear of the carriage to the brightest star of the sky.

»Because where the shaft of the small carriage starts, this is the Pole Star,« as a result I spoke.

It was a day when the new moon had appeared particularly bright the stars, a day where the starry sky as the romantic backdrop was suitable particularly well.

10. Actually,
everything should be good

Our common time was the nicest what I could experience and it was to be known wonderfully that you were there. Over and over again I see your gentle smile which your lips dribbled round, met moments in it our looks and joined in quiet arrangement our thoughts.

An irony of our words that we both used with the knowledge that the other person understands and even answered.

We made to ourselves mutually fine compliments which sometimes caused embarrassment, but with pleasure were accepted and over and over again conjured a smile on your face.

We were happy and had everything. I had found even a new job to lead a smaller department in a small business. It is a good company, everybody takes care nicely and, nobody blasphemes the boss, actually, a good sign and the coal was also right.

The flat or the house, you had furnished affectionately and your decoration brought a special style and character in our home.

We were extremely contented with ourselves and the environment had a common flat, touch the nearness promised, unconstrained fatuity we shared. Our embraces gave more than we would have ever thought it; if talks led in different directions, some profoundly, others playful, were also pensive, however, they and stupid. We had a lot of fun and before all, we had ourselves. I felt secure so properly.

One day you complained about pain in the area of the back. Immediately we consulted a doctor him a hemorrhoids ascertained. Colors mood-lightening painkillers provided for an around care and it seemed in such a way as if you were better. However, I saw in your expression that pains tormented you further.

Worries I came along because you always tried to suppress pain. I know, you did not want to load me with it. Though I suffer with you because I feel the morbid behavior as the first and endure, however, one should not consider something so as a load. Rather it would be a load if one looks at it as a personal thing and hides it towards his partner.

Again I heard quite a quiet one groaning and immediately my look at you, the thought was directed what could have it with pains on itself. However, any discussion about that always run immediately and this ate again in me.

We visited the second practice. Here we sat in a waiting room, with especially quiet silence. Nobody said something, nobody might move, because one would pull, otherwise, the looks of the others on him what could cause a strong feeling of the control.

If one has, however, nevertheless, the courage and takes to himself bravely a magazine of the pile, one receives as a man basically the picture of the woman, while granny Gerda leafs round the sports magazine. Then rom shame about the false clutch one acts in such a way as if one is completely deepened in the reading looks the colored pictures and studies the recipes.

The speech hour help called us to the doctor, a man his qualities to me more capable seemed, those of the last doctor. He had examined you in detail and had ascertained a supposition which he could not found closer. To come to an absolutely sure diagnosis, therefore, he had a transfer in a clinic arranged. There a fabric test which should give more explanation about the suffering should be taken out patiently.

At that time one makes to himself no serious thoughts what could be if one is sent in the hospital and because one goes out from a quickly curative health promotion, we still went on the same day in the hospital to lead a preliminary talk and to agree on an appointment.

Then two days later the intervention was carried out. Moments of the waiting, the unawareness, the faith and hope were not to be known what could cause a fabric test for results. During this time not only swearing is announced, but one becomes also impatient and quick to the chain smoker.

In the next week the shattering results. Frightening news which felt like a blow in the face, as if one had faced Regina Halmich, as if to three teeth were pulled without anesthesia. An evil record epithelium in the crossing of the rectum was ascertained, a tumor.

You felt a bitter disappointment, a miss, a defeat, as if suddenly all hopes for the futures were destroyed. Is generated a radical negative experience which can lead not only to resignation but also resignation.

Tears ran through your cheeks and I could do nothing else, than to catch them with the fingers.

I embraced you, my great love, could catch no clear thought, transfer only my physical sensation to you and snuggle up to you.

Comforting words were spoken of the doctor who held a healing by means of radiotherapy and an in addition supporting chemotherapy for adequate with which the DNA of the tumor cells should be brought to the decease.

A glimmer of hope whose shine we did not allow to cool off.

Every day I drove you to the radiology, suffered with you if the radiotherapy was carried out and held you in the arms if the chemotherapy had weakened you.

Two months later the therapy was to an end and a computer tomography was necessary to examine the success of the treatment. The result was evaluated immediately and still on the same day we received the communication that the cancer was defeated.

It was the nicest news which I had one day received. I could have burst into tears with joy and also you seemed to be all at once the happiest person. It is, as if one jumps on a cloud tram Pole or scales on a wonderful summer day a rainbow and slides down him.

»Come lets us drive somewhere, stroll, celebrate, something make,« I spoke.

»A little bit from what becomes warm,« was your proposal. Yes you were already thus a small sensitive to cold person, have felt finest if we lay before the chimney and he emitted at least forty degrees of warmth.

»A hot bath?« I suggested. You looked at me and caught to your head violently and decisively to shake, like an African elephant who waved to himself this the dust of the ears.

»I still know what a lot of better from what to us becomes warm.«

»Really? Question me what this could be fine?« I noted a little bit surprised.

»Hm!« you nodded and pulled, besides, your eyebrows upwards.

»Dancing what you hold from dancing?«

»Do dance?«

»Yes dancing, a sport where muscle construction, motor activity, coordination and balance sense is promoted and becomes warm.«

»I have been earlier in the holiday's camp a really clog dancer,« I reported proudly what you reacted quizzical to:

»Whom it interests that you have hopped on holiday in clogs.«

»Not hopped, danced. The right word is dancing, my treasure, dancing.«

»In clogs? OK, today we go for dancing. But in right shoes!«

»Today?« I to ask allowed.

With a little bit bitter look you looked at me and meant:

»Say only, today you plan something else.«

»N-o, today we go for dancing and tomorrow I maybe plan something else.«

»You do not seem to be glad really about it,« you ascertained.

»I am procured only a little bit.«

»Why you are procured?«

»Today, well, …, we go dance … and tomorrow the feet and hips hurt you because I stepped to you with the tango always on the feet and tried with the hot samba with the wrong hip-swing to impress you.«

Rest entered. Your eyes were far opened, the eyebrows were lifted and your mouth was easily opened.

»Around excuses you are not move.«

»Well, I should have said that I nothing to pull has?«

Your face looked so alive all at once, so impulsively. You bent forwards and spoke in a quiet almost incomprehensible tone:

»One has said you already once that you are an idiot?«

»Yes,« I answered. »You …, now and again.«

Our living together was crowned by butterflies in the belly, tender affection and a lot of romanticism, from recognition, tenderness, understanding and allowance. It was love connected us which became a part of our life. We put together everything, went through thick and thin, fitted simply perfectly to each other, were absolute congenial.

Some maintained even that one would have planted magnets in the hands to us because it no moment gave where we did not march hand in hand by the area.

Every six months a computer tomography was carried out, a medical early diagnosis measure for the prevention of some illnesses.

»I am afraid,« you said every time.

»You do not need this, my treasure,« answered I and was of confident things

»But if they find now, nevertheless, what?«

»You will find nothing! I have said you this up to now before every investigation and have they found what?«

You considered, thought to the past investigations and said after fairly long time:

»One.«

»If you see.«

With my heart and my thoughts, I was every spot with you in this tube, held your hand and tried to take from you the fear.

However, after imaging, again and again the pleasing news was that found nothing.

Three weeks later, the pitiful warning signals of your body which reached up to the unbearableness became apparent again.

A pain, an unpleasant pain at the same places us previously.

Another biopsy had to be carried out, another fabric test by the pathologist microscopic had to be examined and led to a result which none of us wanted to hear. Small nests of a flat epithelium carcinoma have formed which with sufficient safe distance had to be removed to the healthy fabric.

Questions appeared for what a computer tomography of use is if such wilful fabric educations are not recognized, or such machines are recently served only by dilettantes. Are people today only potential objects for the doctor, to help his hip okra tables oath people has forgotten, because otherwise his valuable source of revenue is lot?

A reduction of the bowel had to be carried out, because the nests were too big around them only with radiotherapy to fight. In himself collapsed you sat there, tears ran through your cheeks, deep desperation tore in your heart. It was quiet, a silence of full grief, burnt-out and blank.

I took you in the arm, cuddled up quite firmly to you, glided to you affectionately through the hair and thought of the radiologist who had recently issued a betrayal of the health. My faith in some thesis takers got lost all of a sudden.

Now unreserved nearness was more important than ever to show you my understanding and to stand by you in every situation, to show simply that I am there that I am there always for you and become his. To catch you, to be tender and caring, to bend me patiently and willing to the will and skill, to cross borders together with you and not only to bind ropes to knot, but to melt us on and on to trusting partners.

The conversion of your life habit, the change of your body was not easy for you, I knew this. I knew you, as usual only your mother knew you if she had changed the nappies to you.

Over and over again you told that one had mutilated you that you are only half a person, no these were not you, not for me. I love you, I love you still like on the first day.

Every day I had visited you in the hospital, sometimes even twice a day, in the morning before work and again after work. Often I even brought food with to surprise you, this time even something from McDonalds.

Your eyes watched this happen, as I put the bag on the table, napkins distributed and your often brought for you appetizing hamburger revealed.

»I cannot remember at all that I had ordered what of McDonalds,« you mentioned, while I still got the chips from the bag and deposited them in the middle on the table.

»Are the hamburger …,« you asked, sat down, besides, took chips and spoke crouching down further:

»… and that cheeseburger?«

I got out of another bag two To Go mugs, full with milk shakes, opened the lid and put you.

»Nevertheless, you are up to something,« you asked.

»However, maybe it is also that I am hungry and would simply like to eat with my treasure together.« if I answered.

Absolutely in reality I was up already to what, wanted to deflect you simply a little from your sphere. I know like it is if one has time the whole day to think about him and the diagnosis.

After dismissal from the hospital, became for the case the tiny cancer cells not appreciative for the eye were overlooked, radiotherapy arranged. It was to be exhausted importantly all possibilities, so that your quality of life is restored. Thus I drove you also this spot every day to the radiology.

I was glad that my boss raised so much understanding for my situation and I could exercise my job also half the day. Though the money became scarce, but this was not important, wanted to be there, finally, always for you, you supply, is appealing to you and constantly are available to you. You should know if you need me, I stand quite close beside you.

At last it was determined that we tired ourselves above the way and that our circle had shut bit by bit. Love is, finally, no sofa cushion on which one can rest but to prove the ability every day anew.

11. You said not even farewell

The time passed, you got used so slowly to your physical change and I was ready always with pleasure help for you with your care.

»Hand from, this is my job,« I always argued when you tried to jam the signal to me while putting on the Ostomy.

»Nevertheless, I only want to help you,« was your objection, besides, watched with far open eyes how I took care.

»You do not need this, does already only. Finally, I do not make it for the first time. So yet firmly press and then it is OK.«

»Thanks,« I heard saying every time quietly.

A wonderful present which expresses recognition for something given and achieved and edges out negative and incriminating feelings and thoughts; the satisfaction, fallen, joy and enthusiasm reveals.

However, with you these were anxious, grievous and clouded thanks over and over again. Not that you had not said it with pleasure, no, it was rather you because of your physical change with the problem of the nursing need got into contact that you did not feel quite fine anymore and had won the impression to depend on the help more different.

However, this is not in such a way. I did it with pleasure because it was a self-evident fact for me and because I love you.

You gave me afterwards always a kiss on the mouth, spread with it a positive feeling of the admiration and it was for me of the thanks the nicest wage.

However, you were not anymore the "old person", the fun-loving, scoundrel-like, quizzical and roguish woman as I had got to know them, nevertheless, I loved you about everything. I simply did not want to lose you because we simply belonging together, in good ones as well as on bad days.

These were pains which changed you and tormented which warned the body about some menacing fabric damages. They must be treated expertly, before the pain feeling digs itself in in the brain.

The visit of a pain therapy was necessary therefore, a remedial method the supposedly stopping pain freedom promised. A whole series of analgesic preparations, up to opiates, to active substances similar to morphine, were given. However, it did not bring a lot.

Depressive phases resulted, caused by the chronic suffering, by compulsions, fears and sleeplessness. They affected your life, your body, your feelings; you're thinking and action, however, not my love to you.

The psychic dejection further spread out not to know linked with a dejection what brings the health future with itself. Self-reproach and feelings of guilt tormented you, brought a negative picture, called the life pointless and you believed to never again be able to become happy, never mind healthy. With words:

»Darling, we still have so many years before us. Think of our vacation the next year, to our dance hours, to the adventures and surprises which waited for us, on the common future which still lay before us. Think a little positive.«

Positive thinking reminds me of what we have already experienced everything and what was well in our life.

I tried to deflect you over and over again with words of your low to bring you on other thoughts to cheer up you simply a little. Sometimes I had the feeling, I had created it. However, then you spoke again words which shook me totally:

»I believe it is better if you search a new woman for yourself.« Besides, you held on my hand in such a way as if you wanted never again to give them.

I did not know what I about it should hold. For many years we are together and over and over again you had said me that you love me and which I would be yours one and everything. I could not simply accept your opinion groundless for me because I did not hold them for Plausible.

»Darling what I have to do with another woman I has you, I want no one else.«

»Nevertheless, I am only one load for you.«

I took you in the arm, pressed you quite firmly to my breast, kissed your hair and spoke:

»Where did you get the silly idea of being a burden? Darling I love you and, therefore, it is natural for me to give you my whole attention. If I was ill, you would do the same also for me, I know this.«

Also during your stationary psychotherapy, I had visited you every day, have been with you pint, walk and eat gone, has blathered for hours with you, was always near you.

Hand in hand, side by side and with a cheered up smile we went every time once more together a piece; and I knew with certainty that if our ways should separate, they will also find themselves.

Then one day I will never forget. By an investigation with an ultrasound scanner it was found out that metastases had formed in the liver.

How something like that can happen, I asked myself. Just recently one of these computer tomography examinations had taken place again and it was found nothing. If it is due to the fact that one analyzes for "reasons of the thrift" only the restricted body place of the surgical intervention, although everybody knows that cancer cells walk and settle at other places. If the operation has been carried out by sloppy doctors or they all recently walk around only with blinkers.

In most media it was already publicized, that by the fact that the liver shows a sort of blood filter that it is concerned relatively often by metastases. Why such organs are not regularly examined with?

How you had to have felt when you would receive this news. I got fear; fear that you do not finish the situation. You had bunkered tablets, I had noted it and had hidden them because I feared and you would do what to yourself. No so your life should not end, there must still be a possibility to make you again healthy, finally, I still need you.

Though the liver is one of the most important organs of the person because she fulfils different functions, camps down comparably with a factory which produces a lot a lot and a lot in the balance holds; however, it is to be removed no problem a part of the liver if the rest can be thereby received healthy.

We were moved by another investigation in another shock. The metastases were progressed too far.

Resignation spread from, a capitulation in in view of a felt hopelessness. Hope dwindles that in the diagnosis something else could change.

Again I feel fear which paralyzed me and blocked and again you spoke of looking around me after another woman who is healthy and shows no load. It hurt me to hear such words from you. Besides, I would not like to miss your presence in my life any more. Finally, until you the other ends of the bridge which connected our both hearts.

»Do you see this ring?« I asked and pointed at the ring finger of my right hand. »He seals not only our special love, no he also encourages our mutual promise of the loyalty and by his round form he shows an expression of eternity.«

You looked at your hand, started to turn with thumb and forefinger of the left hand your ring the finger and spoke:

»Yes, but it will never become any more so.«

»Have patience, now you may not surrender. There is still a possibility, waits, you become healthy again.«

»Oh Darling, this you say every time. I do not think that it still becomes what with me.«

»Even if we must endure maybe still something,« I spoke, »so it will be worthwhile, believing to me.«

»At that time you have also said that one finds nothing and what was ...?

You were right, I have said it because I wanted it in such a way because I expected it because I had wished it so much,... for you, for myself.

Some days later we had an appointment in a hospital where an interdisciplinary doctor's team with radioactive hardly recognizable with the naked eye, globules goes forward against metastases in the liver. In contrast to a customary radiotherapy, the metastases not from the outside, but the liver are irradiated with this selective internal radiotherapy directly from the inside with these small globules.

A glimmer of hope! An internal confidence that now everything will turn to the good spread out with me. The faith in the curative effect and the readiness of the recovery, combined with a positive expectation, came to the development.

I saw myself again laughed as we made nonsense, roguishly, clownish almost quite childish; how your hand mine looked and found every time. I felt your simple touch to which I attached so much meaning; the words which you could underline especially affectionately; by virtue of which you gave me if I needed them; the consolation if what went for me too near. However, the light clouded.

The Sirt-therapy could not be applied; the metastases were already too big. It was a shock, as the feeling of a threat, a fear, and a slap in the face. All my hopes dwindled in seconds. It was of the faith in the future which was destroyed within the fraction of one second which allowed to wasting away my last hope.

You took up the communication quite calmly, this surprised me and I got retime fear, infernal fear, menacing fear for the uncertain, for the unpredictable, for our common future. Thoughts circle me; thoughts about the worst what could come up to me; to lose perfidious fearing, a beloved person.

This injustice, two loving people in this kind is to be got apart infamy.

Over and over again I confessed to you my love and many years to us still approached, only to suppress simply my own loss fear.

»I love you so much,« you had always said and I have heard it always so with pleasure because I know how we felt each other.

»I love you also, my treasure.« Yes I loved you really from whole hearts and I could not fancy a life without you at all. I tried to read to you every wish in the eyes, cooked every day for you, baked cake, bought your little favorite rubber bears to you and sat for hours in your bed, while you slept.

You had hardly left the bed, had slept a lot, for myself to the advantage, because in the time I could follow my job which I neglected more and more. My boss still showed understanding. Though I had given up my leading position long ago, however, my work could do half the day further.

Every day I went shopping, cooked with fresh ingredients and brought always to you something tasty, some roughage empire. You had to come again on the legs, I had planned for this, shopped food supplement means which I mixed secretly under food, however, your appetite became lower from day to day.

Sometime I cooked free of charge, you poked around only with the fork in food. By the spoonful I mixed the food supplement means in your coffee, however, and then you also took no more drinks to yourself.

Constantly I sat still in the sitting room and howled with myself, secretly and quietly. You should get from my pain nothing, from my sensitivity, from my delicacy. I would become a leg, an arm and still a lot give more if I knew by the fact that you would become healthy.

Like every morning I got up and cook as first for myself coffee. However, before I always came round the bed to give you your good morning kiss.

You had called "little kiss," demanding if I wanted to creep sometimes from the room because I thought you would still sleep deeply and firmly.

However, this morning was different.

I thought of ours about ten-year-old being together; to the common characteristics and experience to us have welded together; to the blessedness to have values of the same kind and life aims; to our unconditional talks about big subjects of the life which each of us understood and with which they were in good hands.

In every partnership it comes sometime to frictions, however, not with us. We did not know something like that and even conflicts which should be solved very constructively, never appeared with us.

You had yours "Oh no, this say I you rather not" mesh for you discovered to receive the tension of a respect with small secrets. However, you could never keep secrets for yourself and to guess them, was like in an open book to read, mostly.

Our respect became more stable, the greater and more variously the common plans were no matter whether it concerned the everyday need, to the vacation or the purchase of a freehold flat abroad.

We were always together, had had even for some time the same employer. Some called us already Siamese twins because one nowhere saw us sometimes alone. Together we wanted to become old and in my head a dream brightly in love of a lifelong living together version appeared over and over again. Our love just distinguished itself by the fact that we could completely get involved in the other.

However, tomorrow as said, this was different.

You had left me and I stood there and was suddenly alone, only without you. You have jumped on the goods train of the dead's and have come along on a long trip, on a long trip without me.

Tears ran to me through the face. These were tears of pain, the grief, the helplessness, the fear and the feeling of deep insult and injustice.

12. My life as a shadow

Months passed and meanwhile I had caught myself something, at least externally. Internally everything hurt of course still incredibly, but I tried to let make a note of nothing. However, the head cinema held ready special images which allowed asking me over and over again, why. Why you have gone, although it was too early, nevertheless. Always I had to think of you and put to myself the same questions over and over again without receiving a sufficient answer.

For me has broken more than only one world, for me it is, as if to me with living body the heart was torn out and now I did not try to bleed to death. From the outside it will heal with the time quite slowly, however, inside a deep wound will always remain.

Almost every evening I sit before your picture and we talk, speak of things which made us stronger and more stable.

If you still know, completely at the beginning when we interpreted the word no quite differently. You wanted to be on this day for yourself; however, I had the need to want to feel your nearness.

Thus I drove to you, rang in your door,

however, you did not seem to be at home. Where you could be at this late time, I considered. If you meet up with a friend, walking along the mall, or do you visit a cocktail bar? If you hit you might with a strange man? I felt little jealousies climb up in myself break, actually, ideal means around a respect if she too is in high spirits.

However, my jealousy kept to a certain extent, particularly as I owned an affirmative self-esteem. I had given you any trust, all hopes, my dear ability and life ability because I loved you because you were important for me and because I wished that it will go well to us.

An unknown one had quoted sometimes in magazines:

In the sea of the love you can swim only if you are ready to file all fears – above all the fear of the drowning.

How right he has. Suddenly I heard behind myself your voice:

»Nevertheless, I had said that I have today no time.«

»Oh Excuse me, I had understood that you would have today only time for me and which we to us one.«

I interrupted my sentence, noticed that something with you not was right and hacked after:

»What is wrong?«

»This does not deal the least with you,«
you believed.

»I had not asked this,« I answered.

You rummaged meanwhile in your
handbag, got out a key alliance, opened the
door and we went in. I wanted to take you
in the arms; however, you had wound
elegantly from the situation.

»If you do not want to say me what is
wrong, then I can still have a look at your
today's horoscope in the newspaper or read
in the coffee grounds.« if I spoke as a
result.

»What has the word *no* on itself that men
do not want to understand this.«

»If this is called all men or only I,« I
replied to you.

»An old school companion had called.«

»And this old school companion has not
understood the word *no*?«

»No, unfortunately, not.«

I considered, tried with a rhyme from it
acts make what could have it with the old
school companion on itself.

A former connection which suddenly

appears in the new shine? Was the old school companion one more subject for you?

There it was again, this feeling, the event in me that jealousy could release and how an atom bomb can work if one is attacked by bad thoughts.

However, I edged out it, talked myself that the connection only an attachment from old, common spent days is due. At last you have loved each other and have divided a lot what one cannot stroke so simply by memory. Nevertheless, I try to squeeze more out of you:

»I do not get the feeling off that it deals, nevertheless, what with me.«

»Everything not always turns on you,« you had answered.

Ooh, you were irritated a little bit, so I had to steer the conversation in another road.

»Enough from me, we talk sometimes about ourselves. Only so that we agree and in future no misunderstandings appear if we the concept *no time* use, then this is called *no*. Is this right?«

Your eyes squinted to side and you pulled up your eyebrows, caught in to smile and meant:

»Nobody capitalized *no*, rather a written with a small letter one.«

»Now all clarity is removed,« I answered. »Therefore, we have to understand men probably such problems properly what means the female form from *no* really.«

You caught all at once dreadfully in to laugh, this was good in such a way, finally and an unconstrained atmosphere is the best means against strain. Looseness in a respect is better and better than a pinched mood. At this moment I was just very contently with myself to have brought you on other thoughts and thus I further spoke:

»Now where I am already here, you should make what from it. I am right for a common bath.«

You gave me a kiss on the mouth and left the room. I saw to you behind, behind this amusing figure. My whole body caught in to tingle and warmed up internally my heart. You were a wonderful woman, with a pleasant soft voice, an emitting intelligence, humanity, friendliness and a playful cheerfulness.

»If it was or …,« I shouted from the hall to what you came back, held on in the door frame and meant:

»It was nobody no.«

»This sounds good,« I threw.

Yes this was the only spot where we had a small difference of opinion. But our simple difference of opinion had not destroyed our nice harmony immediately. Rather she had created the possibility to mark out the terrain, before it degenerates into a bitter fight which everybody wants to win at all costs.

I still love you and it is difficult for me without living you. I have lost more than only my native country, I had lost you and even being close people cannot help me about this loss away.

Over and over again I put to myself the same questions: Did you have pains when you read out me? Had you longed over again for me? And above all: Were there really no alternatives?

Often I cry because I miss you so much. Sometimes I get drunk even, around the grief of the grief to drown the bitterness which does me in a bottomless insanity.

However, then the next morning I always believe myself as if I had spent the night in the ballast and an intercity express train going about me would have robbed me of my limbs.

With alcohol problems cannot be just

solved, mostly there originate the even other ones which one did not have before without alcohol at all. Only popular head pain reminds of the last evening.

Today is again one day where I visit you. Twice until three times week make I this, on Wednesdays and on Saturdays anyway. My bunch is always bound ready if I stop on the way to you in the flower business. A bird of paradise, with five orange colored roses which should appeal to each of your five senses.

One for your good taste which inspired me over and over again; one for your wonderful eyes which shone every day from new; one for your sense of touch which touched my senses over and over again; one for the smell which your favorite perfume left in every space; as well as one for the hearing that you gave me if I needed it.

The bird of paradise stands for rich coloring and exoticism, as well as for uniqueness, as well as you were it for me. Who gives away such a flower, a compliment makes to the other.

I had surprised you at that time on occasion with flowery specialties of the seduction to reach the triumphal procession on the field of our love. Mostly these were roses, full open land roses, and floriferous beauties with varied smell. You would like them thus.

»Roses are the perfect symbol of our love,« you had said sometimes what I reacted curiously to:

»Yes why, actually?«

You caught in to laugh and your good mood spread over and over again, looked releasing and had a positive effect on me, on my physical condition.

»Because they are incredibly nice and…,«

As a result you showed me your finger. The thorn of a rose had caused a small wound and blood came out a little. Then you further spoke:

… and quite small a little dangerously.«

I took the finger and kissed the wound. Besides, you deeply saw to me in the eyes and I felt this internal satisfaction again.

Today nothing else is left to me, than to release your place of rest from sheets and weed, to remove the withered flowers of the plants and to give fresh waters to the cut flower.

Then we still gave a hard time an extensive walk over the place which is maintained by gardeners and is improved in appearance over and over again, around a worthy site of the rest.

These were wonderful walks with you which felt so alive; I felt even your head how he leant upon my shoulder. Yes I enjoy perceive you in such a way as I wished it.

Everywhere were gravestones of the unknown people on whom noteworthy details can be ascertained. As a result the effigy of a man on an ancient stone, knows which here a secondary school teacher or even a mentor his last rest has found; a pretzel that of a master baker; the leaders of a chimney sweep or the table tennis racquets of a player.

Our walks led us in the most different ways where stones tablet were to be seen which already outlasted centuries. Some could still go to ruin from a cultural-historical change of the region to reported, other were already of the nature.

»I love shop-window dawdling,« you had said sometimes.

»Yes, wonderfully,« I meant only about it.

»To go for walks by shopping streets with the intention, to look only and not to shop.«

»Really.«

»And how does it stand with you?«

»Oh …, … I find great …, but only with you.«

It was a lie of me, because shopping a horror was always to be moved for me, like a Neanderthal man in shopping centers to stand in the cash and to wait if an eight-headed family wants to pay her month purchase by bank map, gives three times the PIN number wrong and now the product must be booked back. If people at the speed of a land tortoise lay her product on the run tape and hold, besides, still an extensive chat with the cashier if for hours every single apple is examined meticulously after possible brown places to complain in the connection to the extremely bad product with the branch manager.

However, sometime I saw the shopping from another perspective, admired you as you could check off ideally your shopping list without part to forget.

I stopped to the most different article, had a look at them from all sides and partially studied the tips, had been surprised at eatable food which proved rather the impression of a potted plant for me.

Even a shop-window stroll found I suddenly thrilling, hand in hand with you from window to window to creep, to get to know your fashion taste to see what suits for you and inappropriate.

Yes it was already a great being. On the one hand you had something like that fresh in yourself; on the other hand you were a right woman. Sometimes a bit clumsy and my foot trod, then you were dear again and affectionate, was clever and made to you many thoughts, could be dear and support-destitute, rock music and blues would want. You looked pretty, had a flawless complexion, forever smiling mouth, a positive radiation like a film star and you had embodied many beauty ideals for me.

Do you still know when you had to do the first time in the hospital and to you blood was tapped? You asked me whether the really germs with wiping are removed.

»What?« I asked.

»This disinfectant with which they wipe the skin of the puncture place.«

»Is this your seriousness?«

»Clearly! Already what belongs of placebos,« you asked.

»First placebos are the pills and secondly they are given for psychological reasons.«

»Exactly, where from you know that the disinfectant really kills germs. Maybe one should only think that they do this.«

These are the winning arguments of a woman who bring us to men over and over again to the shaking of the head, still I answered:

»Maybe disinfectants are there also to the fact that all germs we exhale, are destroyed.«

»With it you could be right possibly for welfare,« then was your final comment.

Yes this was thus your healthy common sense not to believe everything what one moved forward to you. You had looked at some things with the biggest skepticism, accompanied by a lot of doubts and big doubt. On the other hand again you were gullible, natural and impartial like a newborn child.

However, it was about our respect, you were to you certainly without question.

Many claim our acquaintance that I like a phoenix from the ashes came to you and you had accepted me as the goddess of fate Fortuna. A beautiful wisdom, which I like to remember always come back.

.

13. A fatal accident

Today is retime Saturday, one day where you always got your fresh flowers and where we enjoyed together the fresh air, thought, observed and a lot of time with each other spent.

Mental talks revived you over and over again and this was good thus. Here on the cemetery I am free of the pressure of the society which is exercised on one. Here my thoughts will transfer, conceive, used and answered, answered from you.

Undisturbed we went along of the ways, the cultivated places of rest marveled at, the extravagantly made monuments, the generosity of the site, shamed, however, occasionally to us the grave places which were surprised by the nature.

In warm and on cold days, we went for a walk. Though, particularly by the winter it was already an overcoming if to one after a few steps the feet already froze. But also in summer there were cold days, the so-called sheep cold. But I am no sheep.

In summer the graves are nicely covered with a summery compulsory flower splendor which donate a reassuring and contemplative atmosphere; in winter with cleverly invested arrangements from branches of blue spruces, silver firs, false cypresses and mussel cypresses, as well as from mosses.

The evergreen branches which make the grave not only nicely, simply and cheering but the eye are calmed and sink the pulse.

With a restful relaxation, a free head and a meditative leisure I came along again on the way home.

Still in thoughts submerged I walked over the street, did not notice how a carriage at banked speed shot near. His lamps flashed, sound signals sounded, however, shrieked the brakes too late. Head-on the vehicle grasped me, flung me by the air and dropped me only after some meters again to ground.

As I lay on the roadside and suddenly I realized how quickly everything can change. From one second to the other things happen that change the lives fundamentally. It was a moment where I do not know what to do with me what happened with my thoughts and feelings. Everything revolves around me, the feeling was not going to come afterward. Memories, thoughts, feelings, relationships pull past me, like a movie.

I suddenly saw my childhood, a time where of the 100 DM of light still in the purses of the adults laughed, where the five-Mark coin with Heiermann was approached, where the 2 DM of Max Planck coin were every now and then in chocolate boards which one received from aunts and where the 1 DM of coin of granny was always very welcome when the Hamburg fair was opened.

We made pranks, knotted a change purse with a nylon thread, laid it on the sidewalk and hid us behind a hedge. There were so many beaming faces which became by the expected monetary blessing quite chaotically in the head, however, regenerated fast again when we pulled away the purse.

Then was there the girl who taught the kisses me with my ten years. Man it was quite old, fourteen, nearly fifteen. But she knew everything about the kisses. First I found it peculiar, however, sometime I found fallen in it.

I saw my first real firm friend suddenly before myself; she got to know with 21, was properly fallen in love in them and thus we also soon moved together. However, soon I noted that she amounted to me with her colleagues. An absolute No Go for ourselves and thus we separated again.

I also lived through the time with you once again; everything is more or less identical. Carefully and unobtrusively you stepped in my life. We got on right away, have always fought on occasion the nights over the ears. Tells us things which were insignificant importantly, amusing and also serious, sometimes quite childishly. Then there came the tragic moment where you had left me where a world breaking down for me, one moment where one he any more did not want to live.

Now here I lie, wishes me to pause, to lie just quietly there, to think and to let work the rest on myself. To feel wishes to me again the hand of you if it glides to me affectionately through the hair; to perceive your lips if they touch softly my face; to sniff the smell of your skin which made me addicted, more addicted than one of your favorite perfumes.

Suddenly I heard voices, voices of other people who ran troubled and confused about and presented impassable questions:

»Does he still live?«

»Seems in such a way.«

Another shouted reproachfully in the crowd of people which had collected numerously:

»Call, nevertheless, one the police and an ambulance, but fast!«

Other people interfered with the talks:

»Should we not bring him in the side situation?«

»After we make one, what wrong. I had to learn this though sometimes before the driving license check, but this already dates back umpteen years.«

»The rescue service will be immediately here,« I heard shouting somebody from the amount.«

»Block off the accident place, nevertheless, one blocks off the accident place,« shouted a passer-by.

A woman brought herself with a vigorous tone to word: »Let pass me sometimes, let pass me sometimes. «

To judge by the voice, it was an older lady, possible-wise she had notion of injured persons. Maybe she was a nurse, old nurse or something like that.

I felt like she knelt down beside me, put something soft under my head and easily with its hand slapped against my cheeks left and right. Then she said to me:

»Do they hear me, can they understand me? If they remain quite quiet, they do not move, help is on the move.«

She glided to me over the head, as if it wanted to calm me. Spoke over and over again softy gentle words which worked almost quite anaesthetizing on me.

I understood, but could not answer lay there motionless and felt the warm blood running down my face. All around me all started to float on, I felt somehow relieved, freed, redeemed. Everything felt normal, but then there were situations that reminded me of you and it hurt again.

The energy of my body is exhausted; my life seems to fade away. It seemed as if now my travels silver cord, which had hitherto kept body and soul together.

Then I heard the siren of a vehicle which approached. People got out, doors banged and opened again. Clattering noises were to be heard, how putting up the chassis a carrying.

An orderly knelt beside me and examined my wounds. I felt his hands which touched my body which felt and connected. Then spoke one in a leisurely tone to me:

»Do they hear me? We have connected them so far and will bring them now in the hospital. If they keep please rests, it could become a little painful if we lift them on the carrying. The journey will not last long, then they are with skilled doctors in the best hands.«

They had a first aid carried out to reduce the chance of survival increase dramatically. Now the transport followed the nearest hospital. During the trip, said a paramedic by radio with the control center and the hospital:

»Accident with exterior strong injuries, skin artery and spleen sly, bruises of lung and brain, bleeding in the chest, deep cuts in arm and breast, fractured pelvis and collarbone breaks, strong loss of blood. Suspicion on a cranial brain trauma.«

»Understood, I heard ready emergency operation before« saying still and lost once more the meditation.

I indulged myself in the past, in recollection of my childhood and caught in automatically to smile. These are piquant details present themselves as if they had been only yesterday, the first sight, the first date, the first kiss.

I saw you as a small girl how we played together, on the street before our house; like me started to fall in love me in you without knowing one day the meaning of the love. I hoped that there will be nothing in the world what could separate us. We went for hand to hand every way together, no seconds wanted to be separated of each other, wished that we would never lose ourselves out of sight.

If you see the both there, these are lovers, one called us behind and, besides, we became red. We were still very young, our thoughts freely. Even if this new world was still foreign to us, we were determined in the heart even then for each other.

»If I am big, I will marry you,« you had said.

»And if I do not want this,« I said.

»Then say I that of my sister and then it comes and helps me.«

»Yes and if your sister also does not want?«

»Then say I mummy and dad!«

»And if also do not want?«

»Then I go to granny and grandpa …,«

Thus you were level, Strong-minded, single-minded and logical. However, only many decades had to pass, before our ways led to each other.

In the hospital come I came by the jerky one move the carrying again to me and heard the orderly shouting:

»From the way…, from the way…, f-r-o-m t-h-e w-a-y.«

»High loss of blood, pulse weakly, blood pressure 85 to thirty,« spoke another.

I came into a room whose brightness was so strong that even penetrated the light through my closed eyes covered with dried blood. Anywhere there was a smell, sometimes sweet, sometimes sour, according to disinfectant, urine and bowel movements, after formaldehyde and detergent, butyric acid and death.

»Everybody ready?« asked a doctor.

»Yes,« was answered by different people.

»Then one, two, three and …, off.«

With a strong jerk one lifted me from the bar on the OP table, a hard metallic base. She was cold and frightened me. I tried to open my eyes to see what happened with me, however, I did not create it, was to be moved too weakly generally.

I felt a needle how it was pushed in the crook of the arm, a peripheral vein catheter, an access road for drips; then electrodes on the breast were stuck to me to tape the heartbeat; a clip in the left finger, for the control of the oxygen salary in the blood, as well as an artificial respiration mask to supply to me oxygen.

»Rest,« spoke again the doctor.» See rest please, sometimes like it stands with the respiration. Clear on the left side …, no respiration on the right side, turn round.«

A sister shouted completely excitedly:

»Being blood pressure falls, sixty to thirty.«

»Put them a venous catheter.«

»How is his blood group?«

»Zero positively,« called another sister.

»Blood plasma six units, fast.«

Then I heard a nervously sounding voice of a woman from the doctor's team again:

»He defibrillated,« on which another doctor ordered:

»Revive, fast.«

»Everybody withdraws, 200 joules! Store and …, off.«

Slowly I lost my consciousness again; felt me made easier, relieved from tortures. It was reassuring, eases, comforting, and exonerating, no pain, no noise, no grief.

It became all at once coldly around me, a cold from below in upward over my body walked. My face is covered with sweat, my fingers as deadly. Desperately I tried to inhale, however, the air disappeared immediately again from my lungs. I become worried, feel a strain, talk with imaginary people, however and receive no answers.

My taste sense and sense of smell disappears. Muscles lose bit by bit the ability to obey the will and my body sinks. I stretch myself out long, become more and more tired, a paralyzing tiredness which overcame me. My perception was affected, general indisposition originated.

It is like the feeling to drown. The will fights for the survival, however, the body is too weak. One tries to come to the surface, swallows water, the diving reflex starts, the heartbeat becomes slower, every drop of blood is drawn off and with the last strength one moves the arms as if one wants to stretch in a ladder.

One stops the breath under water, as long as it goes, then one inhales the water, chokes, coughs and inhaled even more. From reflex the windpipe closes mind, the unconsciousness starts and, finally, the cardiac arrest.

In the sub consciousness I heard like excitedly a doctor shouted:

»Two milligrams of adrenalin intravenous.«

»Is all right, two milligrams intravenous,« answered a sister.

»Lung is free, pupils narrows and without reaction, blood pressure further sinks, heart frequency unstable. Ventricular fibrillation,« spoke another. Then all at once:

»He does not breathe anymore.«

»Loading on 360 joules and …, off!«

I felt the paddles which were pressed my chest and the electric shock which should restore my heart activity.

Another attempt was undertaken, however, this time I did not feel the paddles any more. I also did not hear the vibration, the prickle, the shivering, quake and raising my upper part of the body after this surge, any more.

A feeling originated, as if the sphere was not real, as if I stood in the fog, my twill from me would have separated and now I have become sensitively compared with light and noises.

I heard only briefly the statement of the doctor:

»No pulse, he has exhaled. His heart stands still, the entry of the death has occurred.«

I slowly rose, was directed upright, looked down and got a fright when I saw lying myself still there on the table. My body lifelessly and quiescent, modestly and humble, joyfully and cheerfully, a state which had signaled the ending of the life.

A very emotional moment met me, however, I felt at the same time no more pains or restrictions, only one unknown ease, a floating, one pause of my body in the air as a hot-air balloon him flies, how an astronaut in the universe

I could perceive at this moment still everything, the persons present, the instruments, the monitor and vital parameter, could float by walls and covers, and glide through by all obstacles.

However, then …,

14. Welcome home

But then I felt darkness gave to me, a deep darkness, unclear and incomprehensible. She made an ignorance in me will come to what. It was not a horrible darkness, but a good-natured not cold, a pleasant respectable dark. A classic place of the past, where the settlement is directed to the in life has been achieved and where the last emotions can be discharged; where you get into an existential area where there is a social liberation and is where one of the future spaces allocated: in Paradise or in Hell.

It is redemption of the earthly existence and a completion of the life work. However, in spite of that the darkness primarily by the bad persons is used, is not so evil them at all if one thinks that it is due only in missing light; the fact that here no moon is to be seen which contrasts by the radiotherapy of the sun with the dark background.

It is only that one cannot use his visual perception property that one moves like a visually impaired. However, if one thinks that most babies are born at the dark night and this not only with stream failure; if one thinks that the seed of a plant is spent in the dark mother's earth to germinate, then the darkness seems to be quite a normal phenomenon.

I followed the path of darkness, walking against the unknown. In my dismay and in the hope of a reply, called out in the vastness of:

»H-e-l-l-o!«

A sound was to be heard, as if I was in a tunnel, in an artificial tube. An echo, mine shout with more and more weakly growing signals reflected.

With stretched out arms I tried to feel the sides which threw back mine, Hello, as a sound, went towards step by step to her, however, I found no opposition, no obstacle, no wall or such.

After some steps I stopped, believed myself, as if I looked with a cow's mask blind for objects.

Again I shouted:

»H-e-l-l-o, somebody is here?«

However, I got no answer, heard only the vague response of my words. I went on halting and suddenly I heard voices. A choir of the voices was gentle was charming which, confidently and empathetically shouted:

»Come, come to me, and come.«

I properly feel like the darkness more and more around me stretched as my thoughts rush in the darkness and how they try with all the strength to prove me to her.

Even if I saw nothing, something was in me that to me ordered to this voice to follow. Second-long I stared in the endless darkness and asked myself what had it everything with it on itself which see darkness, the voices, nothing.

Looking for the secret of this mystery, I pushed one foot before the other, put my head sideways to the right, to absorb any noise to the left ear better, but it was quiet, very quiet. A pleasant relaxing tranquility, the eerie sounds buried among themselves. A moment for the Spirit to cleanse and get rid of worries and fears, so that I could concentrate on the pure being, to open myself with calm awareness, internally me to unwind from my circling around me thought.

Slowly I went by the darkness to me more and more insecurity, indecision and fear brought, made happy, however, at the same time me with the understanding for simplicity and peace.

It is dark one does not see me and, nevertheless, there are my steps so loud that I got fear, they would betray me.

Quite firmly I clenched my fists; it presses together, trails with the feet quite quietly about the ground, however, the pictures in my head made the darkness even more intolerable.

It is as located one in one of these bizarre objects that are referred to in astrophysics as classical black holes in which to collapse notions of time and space, where matter can fall, but does not fall out again, absorb everything, even whole devour planets and stars in it.

Not to be able to see a little bit any more, to feel squeezed in the darkness, the fear of this ostensible absolute loneliness and maybe narrowness, gnawed at me.

Then all at once a light in the distance, a white light, a light like the miraculous shine of the thousands of glowworms which emitted a luminous concert; how the sunlight of a spring like day that flowers wake too new lives and how the lights of a city, which awoke at the break of dawn.

Round myself I suddenly saw in the light of the bright elves floating, many elves.

They were slim, slender and wonderful, and they looked really young, carried long bright clothes, had to friendly faces and shoulder-length hair which seemed golden brown.

Their hands touched my thoughts which encouraged me to start the way from the darkness of the tunnel in the brilliant light with them together.

Magically drawn I went towards to the shine of the source of light. It emitted charity, warmth and love and did me on and on, against the shining light. It was the way in a still invisible and unknown dimension, one wander through to the sluice to the everlasting life, a crossing from the end of the existence in another existence state.

The light became brighter and brighter, the light more and more comfortably and the feeling in me more and more certainly. Cheerfulness and satisfaction flowed through my body, about the forthcoming entrance of the heavenly paradise; a place beyond the terrestrial time lies; a place where the souls earthly dead live in a world of full harmony.

The fear in me escaped. A genetic primeval instinct of the person whom already our forefathers had if they spent the night in primitive huts and caves and were afraid of it, by wild animals to be attacked.

Also the way to the dentist is fulfilled with many with fear. Thus one supposed that by this put back of the head and exposing linked with it of the throat, an important role played.

When I reached the end of the tunnel, the elves stood straight-lined before me, smiled and worked gladly inclined. Their veils moved in the light wind and around her bodies a warm, soft light shone. Once again her hands touched my thoughts, then there disappeared they and the glistening light robbed me immediately of my sea property.

Drifting I stood there, closed the mouth tight my eyes and waited, until I had got used to the beaming and cozy mercy of the light.

A little bit surprised I looked around, noted that I was surrounded by the fog. A white fog. A nearly impenetrable white fog which worked like a cosmic cloud of dust and kept me the view forwards.

Again I heard the voice. It was the same voice like just now which was so affectionate so softy, thus softly, and expressed big feeling:

»Come, get on, you have made it same.«

»H-e-l-l-o, who is there then?« I asked.

However, mine was swallowed, Hello, by the fog, was to be heard only fraction-wise.

With outstretched arms I groped the way through this mysterious atmosphere which lent a certain depth, width and size by the gradual hoods, this space. Unflustered I let all my thoughts to this smoke sink and ventured forward me without knowing, when and under which conditions I would one day achieve an aim.

Step by step I crept through this obfuscation; his arms still outstretched groping forward.

It was absolutely quiet. No car this drives, no dog him barks, no wind him rushes and also no children they laugh, absolute silence.

Suddenly I felt how my foot touched an object and it started to rustle. Startled I twitched back, went some steps to the back and considered what could be fine it.

I thought of a queue with the bitter bite of the lie that already Adam and Eva enticed to cost from the tree of the knowledge.

Curiously I bent down and pressed, on all fours creeping, for this something, after this thing, this shape or also the thing.

Carefully I proceeded at the head; I felt the hand far from myself stretched and then an object, an object similar to basket. I felt the twisted pastures which surrounded him and thought of the basket of a snake-charmer whose queue dances after the tones of his flute.

Close I held him before my eyes. He was

empty and I recognized him as a classical basket for the way about the weekly market.

However, how comes here to her? Who was before me here? Was he forgotten mistakenly? Is it usual that one takes possessions with on the long trip? Presents for the relatives whom one possibly meets on the way?

Already in old Egypt were given to the late Pharaohs treasures and objects which they had used while still alive with on the long way in another existing empire to be able to continue just there the life, as before. Because none of the rich Pharaohs sat with pleasure on the ground or slept, even chairs and beds were given. Women and also men should look always good, so that one added cosmetics, ointments, oils, greasepaint and mirror, also clothes.

For the care served jugs with wine and beer, baskets with bread and fruit, as well as mummified meat. Lamps should donate light on the long dark way and weapons, as daggers and swords protect against the evil demons.

I took the basket and further went by this white wall of fog which revealed insecurity and self-doubt.

However, actually, fog is nothing else,

than an aggregation of clouds which is here on the ground and by which one marches.

Having sunk just in this thought, I tripped once more about a little bit and a slightly shaking, very brightly and glazed sounding noise originated. A little bit confused I stood there, still wrapped from thick, uncanny fog and I did not know so surely what I should hold of it. Once more I bent down, felt the ground and seized a bottle.

It was a wine, a white dry Chateau Grand Vin, with representative, qualitatively reliable Cuvee from the province Bordeaux.

I knew this wine, had drunk him with you together when I amazed you retime with one of my surprises.

For moved you had held me because so impossible things always occurred to me which provided for detailed topics in your company.

However, you were taken every time noticeably if so mad things occurred to me. Yes you were already a first-class woman, my smaller fairy-like angel.

I laid the bottle softly in the basket and went on. Where one also looked or listened in, nothing was to be seen, except white smoke and nothing to hear, except silence. Slowly and carefully I pushed a foot before the other, Nothing stared in and hears only as a sound signal, the appearance of my feet.

Suddenly I felt that the crackling sound of a plastic bag that I had almost crushed with the foot. I sat down and picked up this sizzling something felt the shape of a shell and the closer I brought them to my eyes, the smell of strawberries the more I got into the nose.

Yes these were really strawberries, a symbol for humility and modesty. By her round conical form and the small sepal they looked delightful and for biting into tasty.

I laid them in the basket and indulged myself in recollections, thought of one our really sensible experiences to be fed on aphrodisiac fruits when in few meters farther it came almost to a theatrical disaster.

An unwanted hooking my feet made sure that my upper body leaned far forward, I lost his grip and let me sideways then fall to the ground had.

Besides, I held the basket far from myself not to break the bottle and to cut myself possibly still in the shards, although …, humph …, this still goes, actually?

When I support myself with both hands on

the ground to rise, my hand touched a plastic-like small round mug, closed with a lid. I took him, opened the lid and immediately a pleasant chocolate smell met me. With the forefinger I dived one in this chocolate and enjoyed afterwards the slightly sweetish taste of her. She is a little thick, but not is too firm, more a tender-melting chocolate sauce which one to dunk from smaller mouthfuls and fruits used is able.

I thought just of the taste of strawberries with chocolate sauce, combined with the fruity flowery harmony of the wine when I noted that the fog slowly resolved.

Contours were to be seen, contours to and fro moved, but gave to recognize no clear picture. These were silhouettes which showed only blurred outlines with the present light.

Slowly they were to be recognized and approach only with the closer, they accepted shape.

Then I recognized the shapes. These were these elves again who had welcomed me already once so wonderfully. They stood lined up in a line and obstructed the view forwards to me with it. With her good-natured smile they were called me welcome and gave me to understand that I have come back, back home.

It was like balm for the soul, words, a reassurance, after long trip by darkness and brightness, my aim to have reached.

The elves rose, dissipated and formed a lane. With her hands they showed to me the way along them in the paradise, with miraculous scenery and happy colors.

Under me a closer carpet-like lawn, close grown with no visible weed. On the sides of palm trees lush and green and full of dates; Bird of paradise with countless beak-shaped flowers in bright orange; clove-like bougainvillea's in flaming violet and strong vivid carmine.

On the other side the glamorous appearance of the lantana flowers with blossoms violet reddish and yellow orange; hibiscuses with white, dark red and lemon cups, besides extremely colorful oleander bushes. Butterflies sit down on the isolated far open blossoms and supply themselves with nectar.

A gecko was seen. He runs swiftly through the warm sand and disappears in the shade of a stone heap around his tootsies before the warm sand to protect.

Behind myself I hear twittering and croaking from many various birds. It was like an enriching piece of quality of life to listen the Open air concert of the poultry. A cockatoo flew about me away to join the song of his congeners

The play still in the ear hearing, I saw before myself the beach, so velvety, fine-sandy and know shone. I knelt down and let him like suction by my fingers trickle. Behind it the sea that was so crystal clear that one could recognize at some places even every stone on the seabed. Light reflections provided for the fact that it shone turquoise-green to deep blue.

A sloop, a classical sail yacht with a mast turned on the sea. It has a white body with white main sail and head sail.

While I observe the sail maneuver, I deeply breathed deeply and feel the salty sea air on my lips, she licks off and feels the aroma of well spicy fish; from the algae which I sniffed up, from steaks with pepper salt crust.

The slowly setting sun still laughed in her whole splendor and the isolating clouds looked as softy fleecy cotton balls which slowly moved from the gentle wind done further.

I looked around myself; saw in not too wide distance a sand castle, an embankment more existent low of sand which fenced around in a certain territory. Small towers limited the corners and carried colored pennons. The embankment to one side decorates with all kinds of mussels which were formed as a heart. On the other side scenery of stones and starfishes.

In the sandy construction a solar island, an Outdoor lounge bed with half-open awning to the shade-giving. A woman poses before it and revealed by the sunlight only her silhouette. The sun seemed by her hair and brought the color from the inside to the lights. She waved, moved her outstretched arm over the head to and fro.

I turned my head, looked in all directions, but there was no one to see. Again, this woman waved whose appearance seemed noticeably strange to me. Curiosity grabbed me who waved at me. Who goes there from afar greets me friendly. Or was it just a reflex? Making known a warning?

Slowly I started moving, went in a semi-circular curve in the direction of sand castle and stole, besides, the sunlight behind her sidelong. She had a thrilling attractive figure, was nicely formed and sexy. She carried a figure-stressed white top with round neckline and charcoal grey Short with lateral white stripes and half-high slits.

When I came closer recognized I this

creature. Wildly my heart caught in to knock, to hit with uncontrollable joy. Feelings played up, let the pulse rise in the extensive one. My whole body caught in to tingle; my heart and a dream of butterflies warmed up internally awoke.

Recollections climbed up, in common characteristics in which bit by bit advance, always a piece further; to the crossroad where one collected himself to the hands and crossed them together; to the love which became true very seldom and became thereby very valuable very much; to the beaming eyes which were let out sometimes warmhearted, sometimes happily and sometimes; to the touch the nearness mediated; to the soft power it was used to stretch in each other; to the security, to the luck, to many thousand things which made me happy.

I saw you, my wonderful treasure. It is, as if my soul just again has met the person whom it can trust completely, me better knows than I myself.

Yes you were then entered into my life, silent and unobtrusive, and from the first second, you were welcome. From the beginning I've loved you and never liked a man had come so close in such a short time, like you something very special bound us, a character trait, feature, a personality, and a character. Again and again landed your thoughts at the right time for me and coaxed so often a smile, even though I really did not feel just then. I was infinitely grateful that you were come into my life and that I have found you again now.

To gears of Cupid who pierced irresistibly my heart with his arrow and which woke love I ran off. You looked even nicer in the sunlight of the setting sun than I had stored it in my most daring thought. Your smile resembled again that of a goddess, your hair shone with the beaming color reflection of polished marble and your garment wrapped up your smooth appearance like a tender summer wind.

Tears ran through my face when I closed you in my arms and fear spread from … to lose fear you again. Then you kissed me and the kiss were so passionate again and devoted that thousands of butterflies to airplanes mutated and climbed up.

Now consuming, missing, the extensive desire for the beloved person, has come to an end.

 Together we will go again the way, in these fields of the late. Even if this other world is foreign, nevertheless, we were in the heart always one.